MUST LOVE DOGS

A DOGWOOD SWEET ROMANCE

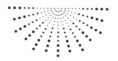

KAREN FOX

PARKER
HAYDEN
MEDIA

Parker Hayden Media
5740 N. Carefree Circle, Suite 120-1
Colorado Springs, CO 80917

ISBN: 978-1-941528-84-6

Art credits:
Cover design: LB Hayden
Couple's feet: Belchonock/DepositPhotos
Dog and cat: valentinar/DepositPhotos

CHAPTER ONE

MEGAN GRINNELL PULLED her Neon to the curb in front of a small two-story house. She double-checked the address against the paper the lawyer gave her. This was the place.

Stepping from her vehicle, Megan paused to study the building. A typical neighborhood house, it was two stories, painted light brown with dark brown trim.

It was a home. It could have been *her* home. With a brother she hadn't seen in almost fifteen years. Her heart skipped a beat. Family.

But was he here? A sense of desolation clung to the building. Though the house was kept up, Meg had the feeling no one lived there. She glanced again at the paper to reassure herself. This was the right address for her father's house—the house she'd inherited.

But where was Riley?

Drawing in a deep breath, Meg shut her car door and marched to the porch. She wasn't about to give up now.

Her heart thudded against her rib cage as she approached the front door. A panel door with small windows filled the doorframe, but the glass was covered by a sheer curtain on the inside. She clenched and unclenched her fist, then pushed the doorbell. A loud *ding-dong* echoed inside, but nothing moved that she could see. No answer.

After a few moments, she knocked. Again, nothing.

Her shoulders drooped. After the anticipation that had built higher with every passing mile of the drive from Denver to Dogwood, the disappointment pressed even more heavily.

What now? She'd expected Riley to be here. Of course, it had been nearly two weeks since she'd been told the brother she'd thought dead was alive. Two weeks since she'd learned the father she'd thought dead years ago was now *really* dead.

Should she call the judge's clerk? She had the letter with that information.

Or should she ask a neighbor? Oh, wait! The neighbor. She'd spoken briefly to the man next door who was watching Riley. He hadn't been pleasant.

She glanced from side to side. Which neighbor? He'd told her he lived right next door, but which side?

Not seeing anyone outside, she sat on the porch steps and dug her cell phone from her purse. Fine, she'd try the judge's office first. They'd know the house number.

She'd only pressed a couple of numbers when a loud barking brought her head up. Her pulse jumped. The phone slid from her nerveless fingers. She leapt to her feet to face the large German shepherd bounding up the front walkway. His terrifying bark preceded him.

Terror held her still as a scream erupted from her throat. She pushed her shaking hands out in front of her. "Go away." She forced the words through her tight throat. "Go."

"Hey, hey, it's okay." A man followed the dog into the yard. "Cutter. Come."

The dog stopped barking, cast a threatening look at Meg,

then sauntered back to stand by the man. The man rubbed the shepherd's head and pointed to the ground. The dog sat.

Meg finally drew in a complete breath. "Who...who are you?" He appeared to be a little older than she, his expression more guarded than friendly. The neighbor?

"I was going to ask you that," he responded. "What are you doing here?"

Meg dared to move closer to the steps, her gaze glued to the dog, who sat panting. "I'm Meg Grinnell. I came to—"

A lanky teenager ran up to the man, focusing on Meg. "Who are you?"

She started forward without thinking. His eyes. Her eyes. Mom's eyes. "Riley?"

The boy frowned. "Yeah. Who...?" He crossed his arms. "Oh, are you Meg? My *long-lost sister?*" He didn't sound happy about it.

As he spoke, the dog rose to its feet to stand protectively in front of the boy, bringing Meg to an abrupt stop.

She licked her dry lips. "Yeah. I—"

The man scowled. "You were supposed to be here a week ago. We expected to meet you at your father's funeral."

Yeah, this was definitely the obnoxious neighbor. Guilt swamped her. She'd wanted to be here for the funeral. "I had trouble rearranging things. I'd been told Riley and my father died years ago." Meg met his steely, cold gaze. "It was a surprise to learn Riley was alive, but a good surprise."

"Yeah, I bet. Now you have a house and a teenager. What a deal." The neighbor didn't hide his sarcasm.

Meg sliced her hand through the air, freezing when the dog stepped closer. "I don't care about the house. I do care about Riley."

She turned her gaze on the boy, who hadn't moved or spoken. "I was seven when our mom died. I missed you a lot for a while, but Aunt Olivia said you and Dad had died, so I forgot. Sort of. I've always felt something...someone, was missing."

"I don't remember you." Riley eyed Meg with obvious contempt. "Why would I want anything to do with you?"

His anger hurt. But he'd been too little to remember anything. She needed to keep that in mind. "Because I'm your legal guardian."

"The hell you are." The tone of Riley's voice elicited a matching growl from the dog, his teeth bared.

Meg's heart rose into her throat as she took an involuntary step backward. "Can we...can we sit and talk about this somewhere?" She waved her hand weakly toward the house. "Without the dog?" She turned toward the man. "Please?"

He must have seen her desperation, for he gave a short nod. "Riley, why don't you take Cutter out back while your *sister* and I talk?"

"Sure." Riley moved toward the gate by the side of the house. "C'mon, Cutter."

The dog glanced at the man, who motioned toward Riley. At once, the dog bounded toward the teen, his tail wagging.

As soon as the gate closed after them, Meg sagged with relief. She shouldn't have this reaction anymore. She was an adult and should know better.

"Cutter won't hurt you," the man said.

She offered a weak smile. "It's a long story." And one she'd prefer to forget. With an effort, she kept her hand from flying to her cheek. Make-up hid the faded scar now.

With a dubious nod, the man motioned for her to precede him into the house. The door was unlocked. If she'd known that...

She paused to pick up her phone—thankfully not broken —and entered. The inside definitely looked like a fifteen-year-old lived there. Shoes and socks littered the hardwood floor of the living room. A jacket hung over the back of an overstuffed chair while soda cans dotted the scarred coffee table in front of the sofa.

"I thought Riley was living with you." The neighbor had said as much when they'd talked over a week ago. Their father had died nearly two weeks earlier. She should've come the minute the judge notified her of her father's death, but Ruxton and work wouldn't allow it.

"Sort of." The man flung a shirt off a recliner to a nearby end table and motioned for her to sit on the sofa. "I live next door. He spends time at both places."

"So, you're Mr. Sullivan?" Her brother's temporary guardian.

He nodded. "Kade Sullivan."

She nodded. "Have you known Riley long?" How did this imposing man fit into her brother's life?

He didn't answer right away, his gaze intense. She shifted beneath it. Why did he make her feel like she was in the wrong? Riley was *her* brother.

It didn't help that those slate-gray eyes sat in a ruggedly handsome face. No, not handsome, but definitely a face to admire. He wore jeans and a close-fitting T-shirt that accented his trim frame. At any other time, she would have appreciated it, but not now.

"Neil and I worked together. I've known him and Riley for over ten years."

"What did you and my father do?" She had no idea.

"We both taught at the survival school in town and worked for Search and Rescue." He leaned forward. "Now, tell me about you. What the hell are you really doing here? Neil didn't have any other children. Not that he told me about." Anger vibrated in his words. "Do you think there's some large inheritance to be had here?"

Meg jerked back from both his tone and his words. "No. No! I *am* his daughter." She sucked in a deep breath to steady her nerves. "Our mother died shortly after Riley turned one. Aunt Olivia said Dad wasn't capable of raising a girl, and took me to live with her. Dad took Riley and disappeared."

When Kade's disapproving gaze didn't change, she continued. "I have a copy of my birth certificate...of Riley's birth certificate." Which she'd only received when the judge's office contacted her.

"And you just now show up?" His doubt came through clearly. "We buried Neil a week ago."

She sighed. "I have a demanding job in Denver. I couldn't get away. Besides, I had to make arrangements for Riley to come live with me."

Kade shook his head. "Never going to happen. Riley's grown up in Dogwood. His school is here. His friends are here."

"I don't have a choice. My job is in Denver. According to the person who called me from the judge's office, I'm Riley's legal guardian since he's still a minor."

Kade's expression darkened. "We can fix that. I was given temporary custody of Riley when Neil died. And I know Riley far better than you. I promised Neil I'd watch over his son, and I will."

"I thought Dad's death was an accident. That he died instantly." A stupid car accident. If she'd only known her father was alive before that...

"It was, but that doesn't mean we didn't talk about things like that."

"Riley is *my* brother. He's my family." Meg rose to her feet, unable to sit any longer. "I'm not losing him again."

Kade stood as well, looming over her. She was tall, but he was taller. Unnerving.

"He's not leaving here," Kade said.

Lifting her chin, she met his arrogant gaze. "Yes, he is."

"Don't I get a say in this?" Riley appeared in the kitchen archway, Cutter beside him.

Meg caught her breath at seeing the dog, but appealed to her brother. "Riley, I really am your sister. I brought some pictures, papers to prove it. At least give me a chance to explain."

Riley cast a glance at Kade, who returned a brief nod. Like Riley needed his permission to talk to her? That would change.

"Fine." Riley's tone was sullen. "Show me."

Grabbing her oversized purse, Meg crossed to the small wooden dining room table. She withdrew the three photos and legal documents the lawyer had sent her. If only she'd had them years ago, she wouldn't have grown up thinking all her immediate family was dead. Her father and brother *had* been there all along.

One photo showed all four of them—Mom, Dad, Meg at six years old, and Riley at about six months. The other was taken a little later when Riley was around ten months.

Riley examined the photos. The eyes, the dimple in one cheek...he couldn't deny it was him. He stared at the front, then studied Mom's scrawled writing on the back with the names and date. Confusion lingered on his face.

Kade only glanced at the photos, concentrating instead on the documents, reading through the one from the judge's office with a frown.

"How did our mother die? Dad didn't say much about her," Riley asked.

Our mother. Meg's heart added an extra beat. "You were around one or so. I think she had cancer. I remember her shrinking...fading away. I know that I cried. A lot."

"So, Dad took me, and this aunt took you?" At Meg's nod, Riley shook his head. "That's stupid. Why would Dad give you up?"

She'd like the answer to that herself. "Aunt Olivia said he couldn't raise a girl properly, so she got custody of me."

Riley set the photos on the table. "He could have told me, taken me to see you. *If* you really are my sister."

"I am your sister." What would it take for him to realize that? "I don't know why he didn't visit me. I wish he had." She'd always mourned not having anyone but Aunt Olivia.

Riley nodded and stared at Meg. Looking for similarities? They had the same nose, but Riley looked more like the father Meg barely remembered, with a shock of curly dark red hair and vivid green eyes. Meg had inherited Mom's looks—though Meg's hair ran to blond with liberal streaks of red, and Meg's eyes changed from green to hazel, depending on what she wore.

Riley finally spoke. "So, you're my sister. Now what?"

"I want us to be a family. For you to come live with me in Denver."

"No way." Riley took a step back. "This is my home. Why don't you move here?"

"I can't. My job is in Denver, and it's very hands-on. I work for a corporate fixer, who depends on me." And then some. She'd been lucky Ruxton had given her time to come to Dogwood on a Sunday. Besides, Dogwood was a small town...she cast a glance at Cutter...filled with dogs. She could never live here.

She tried again. "Look, try it for a week. I have a two-bedroom condo in one of the high-rises near the Sixteenth Street Mall. There's lots to do in Denver. You'll love it." The excitement, the bustle, the atmosphere, would appeal to him. What teen wouldn't like it?

"And if I don't like it?" His tone indicated he'd already made up his mind.

"Then we'll talk about it. See what other options we have." Not that she knew what those would be.

"What's wrong with staying here by myself? Kade is next door. I know how to cook...sort of."

"Do you have a job that covers utilities and the expenses of keeping up the house?"

Riley hesitated. "I help out at Sanctuary once in a while. And Dad had life insurance. I'll be okay."

"Plus, I am next door," Kade added.

Meg shot him an icy glare. He was no help. She focused on Riley. "What's wrong with me wanting to get to know my brother? You can at least give it a try."

Riley glanced at Kade again. Argh!

Kade still held the lawyer's documents. So, he knew she had legal grounds. He frowned and waved the papers. "Can I make a copy of these? Call someone first? I'm not letting Riley go off with a stranger."

Though she didn't like it, Meg agreed. She'd want validation, too. "Will it take long?"

"Not if Steve is around." He gathered all the papers. "I'll be right back. Why don't you two get to know each other?"

Meg eyed Riley. Her brother didn't seem too keen on the idea, but she waved him toward the couch. "Tell me about school. What grade are you in?"

With a dramatic sigh, Riley fell into the easy chair. "I'll be a sophomore when school starts."

KADE GRIMACED as he hurried to his house. He wasn't worried about her running off with Riley—the fifteen-year-old was a lot harder to manage than that. Heck, Riley was slightly taller than the woman who called herself his sister.

He scanned copies of her documents, then emailed them to his lawyer friend, Steve Brunnelle. It helped that his high-school friend had gone on to become a lawyer and practiced in Dogwood. If Neil had done a will with Steve, none of this would be happening.

With the email sent, he dialed Steve and only had to wait one ring for his friend to pick up. As usual, Steve practically lived on his computer.

"What the heck is this stuff?" he asked.

"Remember the woman I told you about, the one the courts say has custody of Riley? I honestly didn't expect her to show up, but she's here and wants to take Riley away. Can you find out if these are legit?"

"That shouldn't be a problem. This Megan Grinnell—her birth certificate says she was born in Colorado. Give me a few minutes to see what I can find out."

"Great. Thanks." Kade knew he could count on his friend. "Give me a call."

"Will do."

Kade hung up and slid his phone into his pocket. He wasn't about to let any woman pull a fast one on him, though he couldn't figure out what she wanted from all this. Neil had the house and savings in addition to his life insurance policy, which, according to Meg, went to her as next of kin. Neither of those things was reason to want custody of a fifteen-year-old. Kade had known Riley most of his life, loved him as much as a father, and even he'd been ready to string the boy up a few times lately.

It didn't help that she was a looker with her wavy strawberry-blond hair and snapping green eyes, but he was past letting the trimmings affect him. She wore a skirted suit that fit her curves, and heels that made her almost as tall as he was. Definitely a business type. Not a Dogwood type.

He gathered up Meg's original papers and headed back to Neil's house. Time to see if she had discovered the joys of teenagers.

He'd barely reached the front steps when his phone buzzed. He answered at once. "What ya got?"

"She's legit, pal." Steve sounded as incredulous as Kade felt. "Neil and Emily Grinnell gave birth to a girl named Megan Eliza in Colorado Springs born twenty-one years ago. Riley was born six years later. Emily Grinnell died from cancer in when Megan was sseven. Olivia Winthrop, Emily's sister, applied for and received legal custody of Megan soon after that. No record of why, but since this aunt belongs to a prestigious Denver family, I'm going to assume it has to do with that. They moved to Denver while Neil and Riley moved to Dogwood."

"Well, crap." This wasn't what he wanted to hear. "So, this woman is really Riley's legal guardian?" He hadn't wanted to believe it when the court had notified him of her existence. He still didn't.

"According to the law, she is. Judge Lerner only gave you temporary custody until they determined if Neil had any other relatives. Apparently, this Megan is it."

Kade grimaced. "Okay. Thanks, Steve. I appreciate the time. What do I owe you?"

"A drink next time we're out."

"Got it." Kade returned the phone to his pocket and stared at the front door for a moment. Not what he'd expected. Maybe he should let her take Riley for a while. The way the kid had been behaving, she'd bring the boy back in a matter of days. Riley had a cell, so Kade could keep in touch with him.

After entering the living room, Kade found Riley lounged back in the chair, his arms crossed, his expression stubborn. Meg's expression was one of frustration. Kade knew that feeling well when it came to dealing with Riley.

He handed her the papers. "Everything checks out."

Riley straightened. "What? She's *really* my sister?"

"Yep." He shrugged. "You might as well go pack. If you're going to try living with her, now's the best time to do it. School doesn't start for a few weeks yet."

"Seriously?"

Kade grimaced. "According to Steve, she *is* your sister *and* your guardian."

"Who I never knew existed." Riley aimed an accusing glance at Meg.

"That's not my fault," she exclaimed. "I was a kid, too, you know."

Riley paused, obviously not happy. "Do you promise I can come home if I don't like it?" he asked Meg.

"I said we'd talk about it."

Kade gave the woman points. She held her ground. She'd need it.

Riley caught her evasion and turned on Kade. "I can call you, right?"

The boy was wavering. The idea of spending time in Denver probably appealed to his wild side. Kade bit back a smile. "Any time. You know that."

"Fine." Riley heaved a dramatic sigh. "I'll try it." He stomped toward the staircase. "But I won't like it."

As he vanished upstairs, Kade turned his gaze on Meg. "What's your address?" He wasn't about to let her go without a way to find them.

She grimaced, but rummaged in her purse until she produced a pen and small notebook. After a few scribbles, she handed him a piece of paper. "I assume you have my phone number."

"Yeah." He had that much from the courts. "You called me, so you have mine. If you're too busy to bring him back, call me. I'll come get him."

"What if he likes the city?" Her tone was defensive.

"He won't." Riley might think some time in the big city

would be an adventure, but he'd want to return to his home. Kade would put money on it.

"You might be surprised." Meg gathered up her photos and papers. She raised her chin and met Kade's gaze. "This is important to me."

"I'm sure it is." He drew closer, just enough to catch an enticing hint of vanilla. "But you have to remember he's a teenage boy who's recently lost his father. Riley was in the accident, too. He got out of it with small cuts, but his father died. He's had enough change in his life for a while."

Meg nodded, sympathy crossing her face. "I'll remember. I can't mourn a father I didn't really know, but I do remember losing Mom."

At seven years old, no less. That had to have been rough. "It might help Riley to get away for a week or so," he said.

"Or more." She produced an impish grin that landed a sucker punch to his gut. Darn, she was cute.

Riley rumbled down the steps, a duffle bag in his hand.

"Is that all you're bringing?" Meg asked.

"I can come get more if I need it." Riley dropped the bag on the floor and went to ruffle Cutter's fur.

Kade noticed how Meg stiffened as she watched the boy and dog.

"Is that your dog?" she asked. Did Riley hear the fear in her voice?

"Nah, he's Kade's. Watch the place for me, Cut." When he stood upright, the dog whined. "Don't worry, boy. I'll be back."

The determination in Meg's eyes said otherwise. Kade grinned. She was in for a surprise.

Riley crossed to Kade and jutted out his hand. Kade ignored it and pulled him into a quick hug. He'd actually miss the kid. "Be good." Like saying that would help.

Riley nodded as he pulled back. "Always. See you in a week, man."

He scooped up his bag and faced Meg. "Let's go."

Straightening her shoulders, Meg led the way to her car, Riley following.

Kade watched her drive away, Cutter by his side. He already doubted the wisdom of letting Riley leave with this woman, no matter what the courts said. Okay, she was pretty and seemed sincere, and her papers were legal. But he'd learned the hard way not to trust a woman.

Still, it would do the kid good to get away for a while. Riley had been a normal, rough-around-the-edges teen before the accident, but now those edges cut deeper. He was hurting—not that he'd show it except through his behavior.

Maybe he should have warned Megan. He grinned. Then again, she'd find out soon enough. Once she did, Riley would be back with him where Neil would have wanted him, and she'd be gone. Women tended to leave when things got tough. Kade knew that from experience.

He'd probably not see the cute socialite again. For a brief moment, he allowed himself to regret that. But it would be better for everyone in the long run.

He smiled again as he headed home with Cutter. Meg Grinnell had no idea what she was in for.

CHAPTER TWO

"Look, this isn't working out." Riley greeted Meg with those words the moment she stepped through the front door on Thursday after a long day at work. Ruxton had a trip coming up, and was always more demanding before he left. As a high-profile corporate fixer, Ruxton was constantly on the go, and relied completely on her to handle every detail of every trip. Unfortunately, that didn't leave much time to breathe.

She dumped her briefcase on a chair, weariness sparking her anger. "How can you know that? You've barely been here four days."

"I know." Riley crossed his arms. He stood as tall as she did and met her gaze directly. "There are too many people here, too much noise. The traffic is insane. I can't stand it."

"You haven't tried. Have you bothered to visit any of the places I recommended?"

"I don't care about the *the-a-ter*." Riley mocked the word. "And the mall is full of people wanting money. It's not like you're here to spend any time with me. I don't know why you even wanted me here."

Meg sighed. She wanted to be home more, to take Riley places, but Ruxton had kept her hopping all week. As his assistant, she was expected to be at his beck and call twenty-four/seven. Before Riley's arrival, that hadn't bothered her. But now... She'd told Ruxton she needed to be home more, but his wants always came first.

"We'll do some things this weekend. I'll take you to Casa Bonita. It's fun."

He shook his head. "Not interested. I want to go home."

"This is your home now." How could she make him understand that?

"No, it isn't." Riley shoved his face into hers. "You told me I could go back."

"Give it a chance." She wanted this to work. Couldn't he try? "I—"

"Come on. You're never here. You leave early and come back late. How is that 'taking care of me'?" He made air quotes around the phrase. "I see Doug, the security guard downstairs, more than I see you."

"I wasn't prepared for this, Riley. Give me a break." If Social Services knew how little she was home, she'd lose Riley for sure. Somehow, she'd have to convince Ruxton to give her more time off. She grimaced. Yeah, right.

Riley's expression remained stubborn.

She sighed. "Wait until the weekend and we'll talk then." With Ruxton flying out tomorrow night, she might have some free time.

"I'm not changing my mind. I don't like it here." He kicked the nearby recliner so that it started rocking.

She snatched the chair to still it. "Come on, Riley!" she snapped. She was the adult here. "You haven't given it a chance."

She immediately regretted her tone when the teen drew back, his eyes wide.

"I should never have come here." He whirled around and ran into his bedroom, slamming the door after him.

Meg flinched. As expected, Mrs. Spencer, next door, immediately banged on their adjoining wall. She'd done that a lot since Riley's arrival.

Meg dropped onto the couch and leaned back, her arm over her eyes. What now? She'd have to work this out somehow.

She raised her arm to glance at Riley's closed door. Should she go talk to him? What could she say? Having custody of a fifteen-year-old boy had never been on her radar.

Her life had been full. Well, busy, anyhow. Ruxton made sure of that.

Groaning, she aimed an evil eye at her briefcase. She had reading to do to prepare him for his upcoming trip.

But first, dinner. The clock read seven-thirty. Still knotted after the stressful day, her stomach rebelled at the thought of food. But she'd skipped lunch.

"Do you want some dinner, Riley?" When she received no answer, she called again.

"I ate." His words were clipped.

She was failing at this. But the weekend would be different. They could go to the zoo or aquarium or a Rockies game. Did Riley like baseball? She didn't even know. After four days, she didn't know him any better than when they first met.

But she would. She'd find out more about her brother. She wanted this. They were family, after all. This weekend would make a difference.

Now she needed a cup of tea and a hot bath before she tackled the briefing for Ruxton. Before she could grab either of those things, she heard a knock at her door.

Now what?

Using the peephole, she viewed the person outside and drew back with an inner groan. Aunt Olivia. Here. As if her day wasn't bad enough.

Meg unlocked the door to let her aunt enter. As usual, the scent of expensive perfume followed in her path. Once inside, she whirled on Meg.

"So, where's this brother of yours?"

"In his room." Meg shut her door and turned to face her aunt. "He's your nephew as well."

"I want to see him." As usual, Aunt Olivia's words sounded like a demand. She and Ruxton were obviously two of a kind.

"This isn't a good time." Her aunt had explicitly told Meg not to accept custody of her brother. If she met Riley in his current surly mood, she'd immediately tell Meg that she'd been right.

Meg loved her aunt. She did. But finding out her brother was alive took priority over Aunt Olivia's wishes. Meg rarely disobeyed her aunt, but this was important. Knowing her aunt had lied to her for years about her father and brother gave her the courage she needed.

Aunt Olivia didn't respond. Instead, she fixed Meg with "the look." Meg knew it well. It said she'd screwed up again, that she didn't measure up to being a Winthrop.

With a sigh, Meg crossed to Riley's bedroom and rapped on the door.

"What?"

His belligerent tone made Meg close her eyes. "Your Aunt Olivia is here and would like to meet you."

Silence.

"Riley?"

Slowly, the door opened. Riley emerged and eyed Aunt Olivia with suspicion. He obviously wasn't impressed by her well-tailored suit, immaculately coiffed hair, or regal bearing. "You're my mother's sister?"

"I am." Aunt Olivia's tone was as cold as his.

"The one who told my sister that I was dead?"

Meg groaned inside. She'd hoped to arrange this meeting a little later. Aunt Olivia and Riley were from two different worlds. Meg had wanted time to prepare Riley first.

"I believed it was in the best interests of your sister, since she had no chance of ever seeing you again."

"Yet here I am. Funny how that works, isn't it?" Riley's smile held no warmth.

Aunt Olivia whirled on Megan. "This is unacceptable. He's rude and has no manners."

Meg reached out a hand to placate her aunt. "I told you this wasn't a good time. I planned to bring Riley by later."

"Later, when? He's been here nearly a week."

"I haven't had time. Ruxton—"

Aunt Olivia waved a dismissive hand. "You have an excellent job with a prestigious company. You don't want to jeopardize that."

Since Aunt Olivia had been the one to guide Megan into the position with Ruxton, she would see it that way.

"And I don't want to be here," Riley added.

"See?" Aunt Olivia spared him an almost favorable glance. "I knew this was a bad idea. You have a good life, Meg. You don't need a sibling you barely know to ruin it for you."

"He's not ruining it!" Meg's weariness sparked her temper. "We're still getting to know each other."

"Meg. Megan." Aunt Olivia softened her voice and placed her hands on Meg's shoulders. "You've worked hard to get here—a well-paying job, a nice condo, well-connected friends. Don't risk that."

Meg released a long breath. Though she might argue

about the friends—who had time for them?—Aunt Olivia only wanted what was best for her. As long as it fit within the Winthrop legacy.

"This is important to me, Aunt Olivia. Riley is my family."

Her aunt drew back with feigned shock. "And I'm not?"

"Of course you are. I can never repay all you've done for me, but I need this." She'd missed her mother, her father, her brother.

"Hey, I'm not staying here." Riley aimed death glares at both Aunt Olivia and Meg. "Especially not if you're considered my *family*." He stalked back into his bedroom, and Meg's hopes dropped.

This was not going well at all.

"Look, let me spend the weekend with Riley and we'll come over Sunday for dinner," Meg said. By then, she might have a chance to calm her brother down.

"I don't want that odious young man in my house." Aunt Olivia turned toward the door. "If you were smart, you wouldn't either."

Without waiting for a response, she left, closing the door only a little quieter than Riley had earlier.

Megan sighed. This was the first major thing she'd done during her entire life without Aunt Olivia's approval. She needed it to work out. Somehow.

She glanced at the closed bedroom door. She hadn't really thought about what life would be like with her brother around. With only a short time to make the decision, she'd followed her emotions, her desire for her family.

And she didn't regret it. Riley might not be the sweet little brother she remembered, but she still loved him. He'd change his mind with time.

This *would* work out.

MEG OPENED the door to her condo on Friday, her head throbbing. She'd hoped to be home earlier. No such luck.

Thank God, Ruxton's flight left in about two hours. He'd only be gone for four days, but that was time she could spend with Riley.

The apartment was quiet and dark. Meg frowned and switched on a lamp. "Riley?" Dread filtered in. "Riley?" She dropped her briefcase. He'd always been here when she got home—to complain, if nothing else.

The door to his bedroom was closed. She rapped on it. Nothing. "Riley?" She entered his dark room and flipped on the overhead light. Aside from an unmade bed, the room looked deserted.

No, oh no. Meg tugged open a dresser drawer. Empty. All of them. Empty. His duffle was gone. No!

Dashing into the main room, she finally spotted a scribbled note on the dining room table. She snatched it up.

I can't do this anymore. Thanks for trying. R.

Meg pressed a hand to her roiling stomach, suddenly wanting to throw up. He'd left. When? Where had he gone? Back to Dogwood?

She had Riley's cell phone number in her phone. Her hand shook as she dialed. "Answer, Riley. Please."

The ringtone gave way to Riley's voice-messaging service. Was his phone off? Unlikely. Out of charge? More likely.

She disconnected. Where was he? Who would he call?

Kade.

Grabbing up the manila envelope she'd left on the kitchen counter, she dumped it out and located the lawyer's letter with Kade's phone number.

She punched the numbers into her phone, anger rising. How dared they do this to her?

Several rings passed before someone answered. "Kade Sullivan."

"What the hell have you done with Riley?"

"What? Who is this? Megan?" His voice deepened. "What are you talking about?"

Like he didn't know. "Riley's gone. Did he call you to pick him up?"

"No. Wait." A couple moments passed. "He did call, but I missed it. I was in the mountains today. No signal."

Her heart skipped a beat. "You didn't pick him up?"

"No. I just got home. When did he leave?" A hint of anxiety colored Kade's voice now.

"I don't know. I just got home from work, too. Where would he go?"

"Not sure. Maybe he called one of his friends. I'll try them."

"You'll let me know?" Her voice wavered.

"I have your number. I'll call." Kade cut her off without another word, and Meg stared at her phone screen.

Riley was gone. Somewhere. He wasn't with Kade. How would he get out of Denver? He didn't have a car or a license.

The bus.

Grabbing her briefcase, she yanked out her laptop and booted it up. Would the bus station have a record if Riley had purchased a ticket? Did Riley even have enough money to do so?

As she entered her login, her phone rang. She snatched it up without looking at the screen. "Kade?"

"It's Ruxton." His firm voice was clear. "I need you to bring the Lancaster report to the airport. You forgot to pack it."

"You said you didn't need it." She blurted out the words, knowing at once it would be useless. Ruxton was always right.

"I do need it. Bring it now to the east terminal at DIA."

"I can't." Not with Riley missing.

"What?" Ruxton's tone was incredulous. She'd never told him no before.

"My brother is missing. I have to find him."

"This is more important. Go to the office and bring me that report. My flight leaves in just under two hours, so you need to hurry."

Meg drew back from the phone to look at it. Didn't he understand what she'd said? Her brother was more important than a stupid report. "I'll transfer the report to the shared drive. You can access it there once you get to Boston." That would only take her a few minutes to do.

"Megan, I must have that report. In my hand. Now." His anger came through clearly.

"Ruxton, I can't. I have to find Riley."

Silence lingered for a moment. "Megan, either you bring me that report now, or you're fired."

She blinked. He wouldn't do that. She'd worked for him as a special assistant for over two years now, given up her life to help him.

"Did you hear me?" Even with the phone off her ear, she heard him.

Megan hesitated. "I'm sorry, Ruxton. My brother comes first."

"You're fired." He disconnected and Meg sucked in a shuddering breath.

What? No. He couldn't fire her. He'd change his mind. Her stomach roiled even more. She did everything for him. Where else would he find someone as dedicated as she?

Shaking her head, she returned to her computer and located the bus station's number. The call proved fruitless. They had no record of Riley Grinnell buying a ticket to anywhere.

A tear rolled down her cheek as she sank into a kitchen chair. Mental weight pressed down on her. Where could he be? Denver at night wasn't a place for a teenager to be wandering. He didn't even know the city, where to go, where not to go.

And she didn't know where to start looking. Riley would try to get to Dogwood. She knew that. But how would he get there? He wouldn't try to walk. Or hitchhike? Would he?

Her phone jangled again. She noted the number before answering this time. "Kade?"

"Yeah." That single word echoed with futility. "Riley hasn't talked to anyone that I can find."

Despair jabbed at her gut. "Where could he be? How well does he know Denver?"

"Shouldn't you know that by now?" When Meg didn't answer, Kade continued. "He's been there on a class trip or two, but not for much else."

"I tried the bus station already. He didn't buy a ticket."

"Is there any other way?"

"The light rail only goes to the south end of the city. Would he try to walk back?"

"I hope not."

Meg swallowed the hard lump in her throat. "I'm going to drive down there. Maybe I'll see him along the way."

"You—" Kade cut himself off. "Okay. I'll check around town before you get here."

"Okay. 'Bye." Meg disconnected, but kept her hand wrapped around the phone. This was incredible, impossible. Three weeks ago, she didn't even know she had a brother.

And now he was missing.

If anything happened to him, it would be her fault.

No! She'd just found her family. She pushed to her feet and snatched up her keys and purse. *I will find him.*

KADE GRIMACED. He didn't see how Megan's arrival would help anything, but her panic came through clearly. She'd come to Dogwood no matter what he told her. And, no doubt, complicate things as well.

Surprisingly, she sounded like she actually cared about the kid. Maybe she did. At least, for now.

This was just Riley being stupid. A little more stupid than normal, but Kade expected him to surface soon. Kade still hadn't reached Riley's best friend, Matthias, yet. Maybe Matt and his mom had gone to pick up the teen. Probably. Most likely.

Who was he trying to fool? Worry nagged at him, too. How would Neil handle this? The older man had always been intense, focused, and a little sad. Could that sadness have been due to the daughter he'd given up?

Neil had never mentioned Megan, but Kade had glimpsed a worn wallet photo of a young girl once. He hadn't looked close enough to tell if it had been Megan.

Kade hesitated to call the local police station. They knew him well due to his search-and-rescue work, but Kade didn't want to start that level of chaos yet. Riley would turn up. He might be stubborn, angry, and more than a little wild right now, but at the core he was a good kid. A smart kid.

A kid who needed to get his butt home.

Now.

25

MEG SKIMMED the edge of the road. The sun hadn't yet dipped behind the mountains, helping to illuminate the edge of the busy freeway. Despite the late hour, the traffic was still heavy, moving slowly south. No sign of Riley. Nothing.

What if he was injured? In the hospital? She should have checked. Should she contact the police? Would they do anything? She had Riley's note.

Meg bit her lip. If her brother wasn't in Dogwood when she arrived, she'd call the authorities. Even if it jeopardized her guardianship. His safety came first.

Riley will be in Dogwood. She repeated the phrase, trying to convince herself. He had to be okay. She didn't want to consider otherwise.

The slow-moving traffic made it easier for her to keep watch on the shoulder. He would have taken this route. It was fastest and probably the only one he knew.

By the time she entered Colorado Springs, Meg had tears coating her cheeks. He couldn't have walked this far. Not by now. Maybe someone had picked him up, given him a ride.

Oh, she hoped not, but maybe he'd be in Dogwood when she got there.

The sun had given up and darkness swallowed the surroundings by the time she arrived in Dogwood. After jamming her car into park in front of Kade's house, Meg jumped out and rushed to his porch.

Kade met her before she reached the steps. One look at his expression sent her panic into the deep end. No Riley. Surprising herself, she burst into fresh tears.

"It's my fault." She sniffled. "I should never have made him go with me. He hated Denver. He hated it."

"It's not your fault." Equally surprising was the sympathy in Kade's voice. He pulled her gently forward until she buried her face against his chest. "I know him. It's not your fault."

He held her in a loose grip that comforted and offered support at the same time. Meg tried to control her sobs, aware of his broad chest against her cheek, his faint scent of pine. She liked it.

Drawing back, she swiped at her damp face. "I'm sorry. I'm not usually like this." And she wasn't. That was one of the reasons Ruxton had hired her. She kept her emotions in check. Usually.

Of course, she didn't have that job anymore—a thought that didn't help stop the tears.

"I understand." Kade's gaze was warm for a change. "He'll be okay."

Was he trying to convince himself, too?

"We need to call the police." She couldn't put it off any longer.

"I work search and rescue for the county. I just called some of my guys, put them on alert. Folks are looking for him."

"Thank you." After a final shudder, Megan straightened and pushed her shoulders back. "What can I do?"

"Stay here in case he shows up. I'm going to join them. I'll leave Cutter...no." Kade half-smiled. "I'll take Cutter with me."

He'd remembered her fear. Meg returned his wry smile. It had been a long time since anyone had given her any extra thought. For some reason, his remembering warmed her.

"Okay." She stepped toward the porch, then turned as a car pulled to a stop in the street behind them. Though she found it difficult to see details in the dark, Meg could tell the vehicle had seen better days. She looked askance at Kade, but he shook his head with a frown. Nobody he knew, then.

A dark figure got out of the passenger side, then leaned back inside. "Thanks, man. I appreciate it." Closing the door, he turned to face them.

Riley!

Kade and Megan spoke as one. "Where the hell have you been?"

CHAPTER THREE

"What?" Riley eyed Kade and Megan, his expression sheepish. "I left a note."

"Do you have any idea how worried I've been?" Angry and relieved, Meg rushed forward to hug him, then swatted his shoulder when she pulled away. "You couldn't wait until I got home?"

"I didn't know when that would be." Riley protested. "Besides, you would have tried to talk me out of it again."

"I..." She would have.

"Doesn't matter." Kade approached. "That was very stupid."

"I tried to call you."

"And you couldn't wait for me either?" The banked anger in his voice made Riley wince.

"I needed out of there." Riley's expression grew defiant. "You're not my parents. I don't need your permission."

Again, Meg and Kade spoke as one. "Oh, yes, you do."

Meg exchanged a smile with Kade before focusing on Riley again. "Do you have any idea of what you put me through? I've been picturing you dead in an alley somewhere."

"Well, I'm not, am I?"

"Riley." Kade's tone brooked no nonsense. The teen's defiance faded.

"Look, I'm sorry. I didn't mean to worry anyone. I just wanted to come home."

He sounded sincere. Meg sighed. "Where did you go?"

"I headed for Union Station. I figured I could get a bus, but nothing came all the way to Dogwood." Riley shifted his weight from one foot to the other.

"So?" Kade asked.

"I got to talking to this guy outside the station. He said he was driving to Pueblo, so I asked for a ride."

"You what?" Meg's pulse jumped. Was her brother really that stupid? "You didn't even know him."

"I could tell he was a good guy." A defensive note entered Riley's voice. "And he was. He dropped me off on his way there."

"Then how did I beat you here?"

"He had to drop some stuff in the Springs on the way. I didn't care. It was a free ride."

Meg closed her eyes for a moment. "You have no idea how lucky you are."

"I—"

Kade broke in. "I want a report by Sunday." His gaze impaled Riley. "On the dangers of accepting rides from strangers."

"Oh, come on."

"I am *so* serious."

Riley looked away first. "Whatever." He brushed past them into Kade's house.

Meg watched him until the screen door slammed shut, then reached for the porch as her knees went weak. "I think I need to sit down." She sank onto the top step. "I can't believe he did that."

"Teens." Kade crossed to stand across from her. "They think they're invulnerable."

"I like the report idea. Will he actually do it?"

"He will. His dad made Riley do them when he screwed up." Kade rested his arm on the porch railing. "You know, Riley really hated it in Denver."

Though he didn't say it as an accusation, Meg stiffened. "He didn't give it a chance. I was busy with work and couldn't show him around. I'd planned to do that this weekend."

"I get the impression you work a lot."

She did. The courts would frown on her custody if they knew how much. Recalling her last conversation with Ruxton, she grimaced. Did she still have a job? "Ruxton can be demanding," she admitted.

"Why did you want Riley to live with you? He called me once during the week and made it sound like he was an inconvenience to you."

"That's not true!" She loved her brother. Wanted to love him, anyhow. "I need to get to know him. He's my brother."

"Being related doesn't mean he belongs with you."

Meg eyed him. His tone held a note of finality. "We need more time to figure that out."

Kade shook his head and paced away from her. "I saw my lawyer friend this week."

Standing, Meg stared at his back. "Why?" Her stomach flipped. This couldn't be good.

"I'm looking into adopting Riley myself." Kade turned back to face her as Meg felt the color fade from her face.

"I'm his sister." His only remaining family.

"I've known him all his life. It's what Neil would have wanted."

31

"No." Heat followed the cold chill down her spine. "The courts told me I had custody."

"That can be changed." Kade's expression hardened. "Be reasonable about this, Meg. Keeping Riley here with the people he knows is better all around."

And she'd almost started to trust him. "No way!" She backed up a step. "I'm not letting you have him."

"He's not a thing. He's a person." Ice coated Kade's words. "Ask him what he wants."

"That doesn't even give me a chance. He doesn't know me yet." Riley would learn to love her. She just needed time. "I won't let you do this."

Whirling around, she stormed into her father's house, letting the door slam behind her. How dared Kade think he had the right to take her brother away from her?

She leaned against the closed door, her heart pounding. What now?

KADE SHOOK HIS HEAD. That went about as expected. But he had to do what Neil would have wanted. The man hadn't known he was going to die so suddenly and so young. Without a will, his house and his son had gone to his next of kin—a young woman Neil had never mentioned, who had no clue how to raise a teenage boy.

From what Riley had told Kade during the week, she lived in luxury in a highfalutin' place in Denver, and she was never home. Once Kade told Steve about that, his chances of actually getting custody of Riley had to be better.

Meg meant well. Kade would give her that, but she was young, and would soon tire of the responsibility. She'd desert Riley in the end, just as Kade's mother had deserted him.

Better that Riley stay with someone he knew, in a town he knew, with friends around.

Kade entered his house to find music blasting from upstairs. Riley's way of venting.

He climbed the stairs and knocked on Riley's bedroom door, then opened it. As he expected, Riley lay sprawled across his bed, his speakers almost rocking from the noise level. Cutter wasn't in the room, and the dog adored the boy. A sure sign things were too loud. "Turn it down," Kade ordered.

Riley didn't even acknowledge him. Couldn't hear him. Frowning, Kade rapped the bottom of Riley's shoes and mimicked turning the sound down. With a resentful glare, Riley complied.

"That's a bit much, don't you think?" Kade asked.

"I like it that way."

"Uh huh." Kade moved more into the room. "You know that was stupid, right?"

Riley shrugged, not meeting Kade's gaze.

"Why didn't you ask me to come get you?"

"I tried. You didn't answer."

"I was on a rescue. You couldn't have waited?"

Riley shook his head. "Jeez. You sound just like *her*."

Kade almost smiled. Wouldn't Meg love hearing that? "You're here now, but we're not done with this. She does have legal custody of you."

"I don't want her."

"Not your choice, buddy." Kade hesitated. Should he tell Riley he was trying for custody? Probably not. Steve had said he couldn't guarantee success. "You need to apologize to her."

"No way."

Kade stepped closer to the bed and lowered his face to Riley's. "You scared her. A lot. You owe her an apology."

Riley grimaced. "Maybe. She'll probably hightail it back

to her wonderful Denver tonight, and I won't have to see her again."

"We'll see." As shook up as Megan was, Kade didn't picture her driving anywhere else tonight.

"I'm not going back there." Riley's stubbornness filled his expression.

"We'll see about that, too." If Kade had his way, Riley would stay here, but courts moved slowly. Kade would talk to Megan later, when she wasn't so upset—make her see the logic of keeping Riley in Dogwood. If she really cared about her brother as much as she claimed, she would want what was best for him.

Wouldn't she?

MEGAN STARTLED HERSELF AWAKE, the strange surroundings of the masculine-themed bedroom reminding her of her decision to the stay the night in her father's house. There were only two bedrooms, so she'd picked her father's room and his queen-sized bed.

But she'd slept fitfully, Kade's threat to steal her brother swirling in her brain. He couldn't do that. There was no will. Her father had no siblings. She was Riley's closest relative other than Aunt Olivia.

And there was no chance of Aunt Olivia wanting Riley.

Meg needed to call the courts to find out if Kade could really take her brother way. What did she need to do to make sure that didn't happen?

As she showered and dressed, she made mental checklists. She had to cut back on her work hours, for one. Riley had mentioned her long days more than once, and she certainly wouldn't mind leaving the office earlier.

But she liked her job, for the most part. Ruxton was

demanding, but he needed her. She enjoyed knowing she kept his renowned business running so smoothly.

Or, at least, she had. What if he'd really fired her? She had some money saved, but not enough to keep her condo for any length of time. And she was *not* moving back in with Aunt Olivia.

She'd do this on her own. Somehow. But Meg needed to find out what teenage boys liked. If anything. The only time she saw enthusiasm from Riley was in regard to soccer and dogs—neither were things she liked.

And he lived on junk food. During his week with her, he'd complained constantly about not having anything to eat. She had a refrigerator filled with fruits, vegetables, and cheeses—things he apparently didn't like.

Down in the kitchen, she opened the refrigerator to scout it out, then shut it right away. New life forms existed in there, the smell still lingering despite the closed door. Okay, what else was there?

A search revealed a mostly empty jar of peanut butter and stale bread. Not very appealing. What did Riley eat?

Probably food at Kade's house. It had to be better stocked than this. Well, she wasn't going over there. Not yet.

She'd seen a café on the main street when she'd first come to Dogwood. They'd have breakfast.

Meg didn't see anyone else as she stepped outside in a brightly lit morning. The Colorado sun promised a hot day, but the breeze off the nearby mountain range kept it cooler for now. Inhaling, she savored the scent of pines, water, and fresh air. So different from the smell of exhaust in Denver.

She decided to drive, then realized she could have walked once she got there. The Blossom Café was only a few blocks away, with several cars already parked out front. A popular place with the locals. That was a good recommendation by itself.

The pink and black design of the booths greeted her at once. Definitely eye-catching. Especially at 7:00 a.m. in the morning.

A busy woman in a pink and black uniform waved at Meg. "Find a seat anywhere, honey."

Several tables sat empty. Meg spotted one in the far corner and hurried over to it. Dogwood blossoms decorated the walls, leading the way over. Framed photos of dogs hung intermittently between the blossoms. Dogwood definitely liked their dogs.

Meg slid into a booth. If only she did. She ran her finger along the scar on her cheek. With no make-up on, she always thought it was hideously obvious. Aunt Olivia made sure Meg had counseling after the dog attack, but Meg still couldn't control the fear that erupted when she faced a large dog.

"Coffee?" The woman from before paused by the table, coffeepot raised, a cheerful grin in place.

"No, thanks." Meg smiled in return. "Tea?"

"Black or fancy?"

"Black is fine."

"Be right back." The woman's nametag read "Betty" and she waved her free hand at the back of the table. "Menu is there. Special today is biscuits and gravy. Joe's biscuits are the best."

That actually sounded good. Meg skimmed the menu. Everything sounded good. Of course, she'd missed dinner last night. No wonder.

When Betty returned, Meg ordered the biscuits and gravy. "With the eggs scrambled, please."

"You got it, hon. It'll only be a few minutes. Morning crowd hasn't hit yet." Betty hurried behind the chrome-edged luncheonette counter and passed the order in.

Only one other waitress worked in the café right now.

She delivered meals to an older couple at a table on the other side of the room.

Meg studied the few people dining in the café. Five tables held obviously married couples, two younger and three older. A young man, evidently alone, sat at the luncheonette counter, reading through a sheaf of papers as he drank his coffee. The conversations didn't carry, and Meg found herself relaxing in the casual atmosphere.

Now to make her list permanent instead of mental. She grabbed a pen and pad from her purse and started writing. She had to do whatever it took to keep Riley. But how to go about it? She'd have to get a lawyer of her own. Fight Kade somehow.

Meg ran a hand over her face. She'd never expected this. How could she handle such a big change? Was she capable of raising a rebellious fifteen-year-old?

"You okay, hon?" When Meg jerked her head up, Betty slid a plate of steaming food in front of her, then slid into the opposite side of the booth. "Go on and eat now while it's hot."

"I...ah..." This was different.

"Eat. Joe's biscuits fix a lot of ailments." Betty grinned and motioned toward the plate. She waited for Meg to take a bite before continuing. "You're new here, aren't you?"

"I..." How to respond to that? "I'm Meg Grinnell. I—"

"Oh, glory be, you're Neil's girl. You've been the talk of the town since Neil died and we learned about his daughter. Where have you been?"

Meg took another bite as she formed a response. Definitely different here. "In Denver. I'd been told my dad and Riley were dead."

"I knew it was something like that. I told Tina that, didn't I, Tina?" Betty raised her voice toward the other waitress, who turned, then approached the table.

Now what? Meg closed her eyes for a brief moment.

"Told me what?" Tina asked.

"That Neil's daughter had a good reason for not being here." Betty waved at Meg. "This is her. Meg Grinnell."

Tina wiped her hand on her apron, then extended it. "Pleased to meet you. Welcome to Dogwood. You'll like it here."

"I...I'm not planning on staying in Dogwood." Both waitresses looked at Meg as if she'd sprouted a third eye. "My home, my job, are in Denver."

"Oh, honey." Betty reached across the table to touch Meg's hand. "You can't take Riley away from his home."

Was everyone against her? "I have no choice."

"There's always a choice." Tina nodded as if she'd said something profound. "Why, the stories we could tell you about Riley would heat your coffee."

"He and Matt, his best friend. Those two—"

"I know." Meg produced a sympathetic smile as she cut Betty off. These women meant well, but she didn't need this. "But Denver is my home."

"That's just because you don't know Dogwood," Betty said. "Folks love it here."

But there are dogs here. Meg didn't say that aloud, though. They'd think she'd grown a fourth eye then.

Tina glanced back as the chimes over the door rang. She placed a reassuring hand on Meg's shoulder before she took off. "Give this place a chance."

"It's not that simple." Meg sighed as Betty squeezed her hand.

"It never is, hon." Betty's hand displayed the beginning of age spots, but her smile was warm.

"Kade wants to take him from me." Meg found herself blurting out the statement before she thought.

Betty withdrew her hand, her expression shocked. "Oh,

dear. He would do that. Kade and Neil were like family. They'd do anything for each other."

Oh, that helped. Not. "But I haven't had a chance to know Riley. Or for him to know me."

"True enough. You need someone on your side." Betty raised her voice again. "Steve, come on over here."

The young man at the counter looked around. "Betty?"

"Get over here."

"Yes, ma'am." The young man gathered his papers into his briefcase, then sauntered to the table.

Meg drew in a slow breath. They sure made guys good-looking here. Tall and lean, this guy sported close-cropped chocolate brown hair and a smile that took up his entire face. He extended his hand to Meg.

"Steve Brunnelle. You called?"

Betty stood and pushed Steve down into her spot. "This is Meg Grinnell, Neil's daughter. She needs some legal help."

"Oh." The admiration in Steve's eyes changed to curiosity. "How can I help you?"

"I don't know that you can. It's complicated." Meg pushed her half-eaten plate away, her appetite fading. "I just found out my dad and brother are alive. Were alive, anyhow." She sighed. "I'd been told they were dead."

"That would be a shock."

"You're not kidding." Steve nodded for her to continue. Was it his sympathetic brown eyes that made it so easy for her to spill this all out? "I love my brother. I want us to be a family again." To her horror, tears welled up. "Is that so bad?"

"Of course not. But I—"

She cut him off, the words tumbling over each other. "But Riley doesn't like Denver. My job. My life is there. I can't just up and leave all that."

"I see. I—"

She rushed on. "I don't know what to do. I can't lose Riley again."

Steve gave up trying to talk and nodded.

"Now Kade wants to fight me for custody." Meg blinked away her tears and mustered a watery smile. "Oh, gosh. You probably know them."

"Actually..."

"Do you know Riley?"

"Very well. I've lived most of my life in Dogwood."

Meg groaned internally. "That probably means you know Kade, too." She wouldn't be surprised if everyone in Dogwood knew everyone else.

"I've known Kade since childhood." Steve produced a wry smile. "Actually, Meg, I'm Kade's lawyer."

Meg's stomach dropped to her toes. "Of course you are."

CHAPTER FOUR

"And you just let me ramble on?" Meg frowned. "Isn't that unethical?"

"I tried to tell you, but you kept interrupting me. Besides, this is good for me. All I have is Kade's side of things. Hearing your side is helpful."

"So you can use it against me?" Meg looked for Betty so she could pay her bill and get out of here. Dogwood was definitely *not* the place for her.

"No. No. Meg, it's okay." Steve's smile looked genuine. "I think we can work this out."

"How?"

"Both you and Kade want what's best for Riley, right?"

Meg nodded. Where was this leading?

"So, we need to put that first and see how we can work out a compromise."

"I don't want a compromise. It'll mean Riley staying here." She knew how this would end up. With luck, she'd have visitation rights.

"Not necessarily." Steve oozed enough charm, Meg was

surprised the butter on the table didn't melt. "Look, Kade is not a bad guy."

"Uh huh," she said, her doubt evident in her tone.

"He knew your father for years. They were great buddies. Worked together for SAR."

"SAR?"

"Search and Rescue. Neil actually saved Kade's life at one point, so I'm sure Kade feels an obligation to watch out for Riley."

"So do I," Meg protested. "It's not my fault I was lied to for years. If I'd known they were alive, I would've been here ages ago."

"I believe you." Steve reached across the table to give her hand a quick squeeze. "That's why I think we can work this out."

"Kade doesn't strike me as the type to compromise." In fact, Meg didn't trust him at all.

"I know him better than you." A dimple appeared when Steve grinned. "After all, you're not the money-hungry city shrew he made you out to be."

"He *what?*" Meg straightened in the seat. The jerk. No way was she leaving Riley with him.

"I like the fire in your eyes when you're angry." Instead of appearing disturbed by her response, Steve only smiled more. He waved at Betty. "Betty, bring me both checks, would you?"

"Just give me a minute," she replied, turning to the cash register on the end of the counter.

"Wait, you can't pay my bill," Meg said. He was the enemy.

"Sure, I can. You're my new friend."

He couldn't be her friend, no matter how charming. "No, you're—"

"How about we go talk to Kade?" he asked.

"Now?" Meg wasn't sure that she wouldn't punch Kade out at the moment.

"No time like the present." Steve stood to accept the check from Betty, then handed her a couple of bills from his wallet. "Keep the change, Betty."

"Thanks, hon."

He extended a hand toward Meg. "Ready?"

"Not really." What did he intend to do? Meg stood to face him.

"I walked here. How about you?"

"I drove. I didn't realize it was so close."

"That's the beauty of Dogwood." Steve motioned for her to precede him to the door. "Everything is close to everything else."

They saw a woman walking her poodle as they emerged. Steve smiled at her. "Good morning, Ellie."

She returned the smile. "Morning to you, Steve."

Meg sighed as she unlocked her car. "Does everyone here know everyone else?"

"Mostly." He slid into her passenger seat.

"And does everyone own a dog?" It sure looked like it, judging from all the folks walking their dogs.

"There are a lot of dogs here," Steve admitted. "After all, it *is* Dogwood."

"Do you have a dog?"

His smile faded. "I did. Sassy passed on a few months ago, and I haven't been ready to get another."

"Oh, I'm sorry."

He shrugged. "She was seventeen, so she lived a long life."

"Still..." Meg had never been allowed a pet, but her friends had grieved for the loss of their companions.

"Dogs don't live as long as we do. Unfortunately." Steve pointed ahead. "Look, Kade's outside. That makes this easier."

Meg failed to see any easy in the situation at all, but she pulled into the driveway of her father's house and killed the engine. Kade approached the car, then stopped when Steve stepped out.

"Steve, what are you—?"

Meg allowed herself a flash of amusement at Kade's stunned expression as she joined them.

Steve produced his infectious grin. "Have no fear, pal. I met Meg at the café, and we got to talking."

"Do you know who she is?"

Kade acted as if Meg was a serial killer. She gave him an overly sweet smile. "He does."

Kade's gaze darkened as he looked from one to the other. "So, what's going on here?"

"Nothing to worry about." Steve's charm apparently didn't work on Kade, for his friend's face remained frozen. "Let's go inside and talk."

He headed for Kade's house, not waiting to see if his friend would follow.

Meg enjoyed Kade's discomfort for a moment. "Coming?" She wasn't sure where this was likely to end, but anything that left Kade unsettled was all right with her. She hurried to join Steve, who held the door open for her to enter Kade's living room.

Kade didn't move for a minute. What the heck was Steve doing? He was supposed to be on Kade's side in this mess. Instead, the lawyer allowed himself to be taken in by a pretty smile. Figured.

With a grimace, Kade followed Steve and Meg into his house to find them already seated in his two living room recliners. He dropped onto the couch. "Make yourself at home," he muttered.

"Thanks." Steve's wide smile irritated Kade more. "We will."

"What is this all about?" Kade asked. Meg shifted at his question. Good, he wanted her to be nervous.

"I got to hear Meg's side of things, which is different from what you told me." Humor danced in Steve's eyes. "She isn't at all like I expected from your description of her."

She was pretty. Kade couldn't dispute that, even with the frown on her face, but she still wanted Neil's house and his son. "You're representing me, aren't you?"

"I am." The sudden seriousness of Steve's expression validated his words, easing the tension in Kade's gut.

"So?"

"I think we can work this out without going to court. Saves pain for everyone."

Of course. Steve was known for settling things out of court. It was his strong suit, and one of the reasons he was so popular in Dogwood.

"What do you have in mind?" Kade was going to hear it whether he wanted to or not.

Steve paused. "Where's Riley?"

"Still sleeping."

"At eight-thirty?"

"He's fifteen." That should be explanation enough.

"Okay." Steve nodded. "I don't have all the details fleshed out, but there has to be a way for you two to share custody of Riley."

"We live in different cities," Meg said.

At the same time, Kade said, "Riley hates Denver."

"Okay, okay." Steve held up his hands. "I said I don't have it all figured out yet, but I will. Give me a couple of days." He turned to Meg. "Can you get back here on Monday morning? We'll meet in my office, and I'll show you my plan."

Meg hesitated and Kade rolled his eyes. Her all-important boss probably wouldn't let her come. He caught himself. For that matter, he had to teach a mountain survival course starting Monday. "Lunch time?" he asked.

"That works." Steve kept his gaze on Meg. "Meg?"

"I'll be there."

Kade had to admire her conviction. Maybe she wasn't as much a city wuss married to her job as he thought.

"Good." Steve pulled a business card from his wallet and handed it to Meg. "I'll expect both of you at noon."

"What about Riley?" Meg asked. No doubt, she wanted to take Riley back to Denver even after he ran away from there. Talk about a dumb move.

"It's probably best to let things settle for now." Steve presented the statement with one of his charming smiles. "It's only a couple of days."

"Okay." Meg didn't look convinced, but she nodded.

Sheesh, this guy could convince the sun to set early. No wonder women loved him.

"Can I at least see Riley before I head back to Denver?" she asked.

"He's asleep," Kade said. Didn't she hear that the first time?

"I know." She responded in the same dry tone. "I plan to get ready to leave first. He might be up by then."

As she spoke, Cutter came bounding down the staircase, his tail wagging and ears up. Meg stiffened as the dog went directly to Steve for some scratching. Kade grimaced. She'd never make it in Dogwood if she was afraid of dogs. Good thing she didn't live here.

"Who's here?" Riley stumbled down the staircase, clad in pajama bottoms and a T-shirt, his hair tousled. He focused on Steve. "Steve, what's up?"

"We're trying to figure out what to do with you." Steve shook his head in mock despair. "An impossible case."

Riley shot a wary glance at Meg. She responded with a tentative smile. "I'm not living in Denver," he said.

Her smile faded and Kade bit back a grin. Steve was going to have a tough time trying to negotiate this situation.

"We'll see what happens." Steve winked at the boy.

Riley relaxed enough to kneel down and wrap his arms around Cutter, sending the killer tail into even more fierce motion. "Not going," he repeated into the dog's fur.

Meg stood, her tension evident in her stiff posture. While she kept her gaze locked on Cutter, she spoke to Riley. "I'm going to Denver, but I'll be back." She drew in a deep breath. "I'm sorry it didn't work out."

"Whatever," Riley replied, not bothering to turn from the dog.

Kade was used to Riley's rudeness, but when Meg flinched, Kade reacted. "Riley!"

"What?" The boy must have recognized the threat in Kade's face, for he grimaced and turned to Meg. "I'm sorry, too." He looked back at Kade. "Better now?"

Kade had to get a handle on the teen. "You—"

"I'm hungry." Not waiting for Kade to finish, Riley dashed to the kitchen.

Torn between following the boy or finishing the conversation, Kade glanced at Meg. The obvious hurt in her expression made his chest tighten. "He's fifteen," Kade said, knowing that didn't excuse Riley's behavior.

"Yeah." Meg offered her hand to Steve. "I'll see you Monday, then."

Steve rose and held her hand just a moment longer than he needed to. Kade frowned. If Steve thought he'd hit on this socialite, Kade would change his mind. No matter how appealing he found her, she definitely didn't belong in Dogwood.

"Till Monday," Steve answered. "Let me walk you to your car."

She shook her head. "I have to grab some things first. But thanks."

She left the house, her back ramrod straight. For a moment, the living room seemed a bit dimmer. Crazy.

Kade focused on his friend. "So, what's going on here?"

"You both care about Riley. That's obvious." Steve shrugged. "That means there's a solution to this."

"Yeah, she stays in her castle in Denver and I handle Riley."

Steve shook his head in mock resignation. "And how's that going for you?" Without waiting for an answer, Steve headed for the door. "See you Monday."

As the door shut after Steve, Kade swore. Why did he suddenly feel as if he was on the losing side of things?

❈ ❈ ❈ ❈

RESTLESS ENERGY HAD Meg cleaning her condo after she returned to the city. Riley hadn't left much mess, but enough so that returning things to their proper places left her a bit more settled.

She debated on going grocery shopping as Riley's short stay had put a dent in her food supplies, even with all his complaints about nothing to eat, but decided against it. She could go tomorrow.

Emotionally exhausted, she fell asleep as soon as her head hit the pillow.

Only to be awakened by the constant ringing of her doorbell early in the morning. Meg glanced at the clock. Not even eight o'clock yet. Who could that be?

Pulling on her robe, she hurried to pull the door open in an effort to stop the incessant bonging. A woman around

Meg's age stood there, her finger jammed against the door-bell. She wore torn jeans and a faded T-shirt for some rock band. Her black hair was cut in a wild shaggy style, and both her lip and nose were adorned by shiny earrings.

"What?" Meg demanded.

The woman looked Meg over, her lip curling in distaste. "I brought your stuff."

"My stuff?"

"Dense, aren't you? No wonder Ruxton fired you." She stepped back to reveal two large grocery bags sitting on the floor beside her. "Your stuff from the office."

Meg blinked. It was too early for this. "From the office?" Her desk at Ruxton's office?

"Yeah, your stuff. Ruxton wanted it out before he gets back." The woman kicked a bag toward the door. Something inside shattered.

Angry now, Meg grabbed the bag and pulled it into her condo, then repeated that action with the other bag. "And who are you?"

"Demi Sawyer." She straightened with an air of importance. "I'm Ruxton's new assistant."

"*You?*" The girl had to be lying. This...this millennial had no professional bearing at all. Ruxton would never accept that.

"Yeah, me." Demi shook back her wavy hair with a sneer. "Guess you couldn't do a good enough job, so he got me. Way to get yourself fired."

She turned away. Startled, Meg scrambled for a response. "You're going to be in for a shock," she called out. No way would Ruxton allow someone like that to handle his office.

Shutting the door, she leaned against it and stared at the two bags. She spotted her desk lamp protruding from out of one. Was this really all her desk stuff?

Meg slowly removed each item from the bags and set

each on the dinette. The shattered object had been a simple figurine she'd bought on a whim from a street fair. A happy-go-lucky elf with a mischievous smile. Not so happy now. Disbelief gave way to sinking realization. Ruxton had actually fired her. Her stomach clenched. He'd *fired* her.

What was she going to do? Winthrops were *never* fired. Aunt Olivia had drilled that into her years ago. Winthrops did the firing.

Meg released a shaky breath. She had money in savings, but with the condo's mortgage and monthly fees, it wouldn't last long. She needed to find another job. Soon.

But she wasn't going back to Aunt Olivia. Meg had been practically given to Ruxton as his admin assistant by her aunt. She hadn't job-shopped at all.

Maybe it was time she acknowledged the Grinnell side of her bloodline. Being a Winthrop had never worked. It was past time for her to stand on her own. A life away from Aunt Olivia might be just what she needed. She was capable and a good worker. She would find a position on her own. It would probably be a better one, too.

Lifting her mug, she studied the saying on it. "Keep calm and get a life." She'd thought it funny when she'd purchased it two years ago as a good way to sum up her job. Now, it was just sad.

If she'd had a life, she would've spent more time with her brother, would've gotten to know him. Family was important to her. She needed to treat it that way,

Meg set the mug down. Nothing said she had to stay in Denver. True, it was all she knew, but her father had left her the house in Dogwood. Riley didn't want to leave Dogwood.

She grimaced. It meant living in the small town of Dogwood...with all those dogs. Still, this was an opportunity to start over with her brother.

New energy filled Meg. She was going to create her own

life now. One with a family. She could do this. She *would* do this.

She went to pull her suitcases from a closet and allowed herself a tiny laugh. Just wait until Kade learned she was going to be his neighbor.

Why did that thought excite her as well?

CHAPTER FIVE

KADE GRIMACED as he approached Steve's office on Monday. Megan's car was parked out front. Considering her busy lifestyle, he hadn't expected her to be on time, let alone early.

Well, better to get this over with. No way did Kade plan to let Riley leave Dogwood. Meg would be disappointed, and a small part of him acknowledged that, but Kade had to do what was best for Neil's son.

Entering the small house that doubled as Steve's law office, Kade heard laughter echoing from the inner office. He stepped inside to find Meg relaxed in a comfy chair opposite Steve, who sat behind his desk.

Steve looked far too comfortable himself, his "woman-wooing" smile in place. Kade scowled. This shouldn't bother him, but it did.

"Cozy enough?" he asked with a direct stare at his friend.

Steve waved him to another chair. "Sorry. Just telling Meg some of things to expect in Dogwood, like our infamous fountain."

"I guess I missed it when I was here before," Megan said with a warm smile.

Kade froze for a moment. He hadn't seen that smile before. It pummeled his gut with the impact of a rock hammer. She should do that more often.

Spotting the answering grin on Steve's face, Kade frowned. Or not.

His friend's words finally slid past Meg's smile to enter Kade's brain. "What you do mean 'expect in Dogwood'?"

"We have the perfect solution on what to do about Riley." Steve waved a hand at Meg. "Meg will move into Neil's house and live there with Riley."

"What?" Where the blazes did that come from? "What about Denver and the job?"

The smile left Meg's face. "Ruxton fired me for deciding to look for Riley instead of taking some papers to him at the airport."

"What a jerk." Kade hadn't liked the sound of the guy before, and really didn't now. With an ass like that for a boss, it was no wonder Meg hadn't come to her father's funeral.

Meg shrugged, though Kade caught a glimpse of a lingering hurt in her gaze. "So, I'm going to try living here for a while and see how that goes. It'll give me a chance to know Riley better."

"I thought you could help her settle in and adapt to having a teenager around," Steve added.

This was happening way too quickly. Kade had expected a major battle, not an acquiescence. Still, he wasn't about to let her be around Riley by herself. "I can do that."

"I plan to show her around Dogwood," Steve said.

"I can do that, too." The words escaped Kade before he thought.

Steve cocked his head. "Are you sure?" Even Meg looked surprised.

Was he sure? Someone needed to supervise this socialite while she was here. It might as well be him. "I'm sure."

Judging from Meg's expression, she wasn't too pleased with that. "Are you sure I'm not too much of a shrew for you?"

Kade grimaced and glared at his friend. Wonder how she knew he'd said that. He'd trusted that spouting off to his friend would stay between them. "Remains to be seen," he replied. She wasn't really that bad, but she was interfering in his life.

"So," Steve jumped in. "We'll give this a few days and see how it goes. Kade, send Riley to stay with her tonight, and I'm sure she'd appreciate any tips you can give her."

Send Riley to stay with her? That wasn't going to go well. Kade half smiled in response.

Steve knew what that meant and turned to Meg. "If you have any problems, just let me know."

"Oh, I will." Meg's reply held too much enthusiasm. She stood. "Thank you, Steve."

"Yeah, thanks, Steve." Kade didn't hide the dryness of his tone.

He accompanied Meg out.

"Didn't you drive?" she asked as he paused beside her car.

"Nah, it's a nice day. My work is only about a mile away."

"Does anyone drive here?"

"Dogwood isn't that small, but most folks don't drive unless they have to."

"The joys of a small town." Her tone indicated she didn't think they were joys. She opened her car door, then paused as he turned away. "Is there a grocery nearby? I noticed the house didn't have much food when I was there."

"Why should it? Riley's been staying with me."

"I know." Meg offered a conciliatory smile as if to ease his defensiveness. Man, she could push his buttons without trying. "I just want to stock up."

Kade nodded. "There's a Super Mart about three miles away. Be warned. Riley eats a lot."

"A growing boy."

"That's an understatement."

"I'm hoping to win him over with my cooking."

"He doesn't care for mine, which is mediocre at best, so that may work."

"Maybe you can join us for dinner sometime." Meg looked as surprised at saying the words as he felt at hearing them.

That sounded like an actual invitation. "Maybe I will." Especially if her cooking was good.

Who was he kidding? Everyone's cooking was better than his. He headed back to work.

Maybe he would.

🐾🐾🐾🐾

RILEY STILL HADN'T SHOWN up by the time Meg finished removing the hazardous waste from the refrigerator and prepared her first dinner in her father's house. Kade was supposed to send the boy over. Did he plan to ignore what Steve told him to do?

Or did she need to go over and get him herself?

With a sigh, Meg covered the potatoes and made her way to the front door. As she gripped the doorknob, it turned by itself and the door swung inward.

She stumbled back with a gasp as Riley and Kade entered. "Ever hear of knocking?" she demanded as she regained her balance.

"Not at my own house," Riley retorted. He dropped his backpack on the floor. "Kade says I have to stay here with you now."

"Yes." Meg swallowed. How to deal with a surly teen?

"Take your stuff to your room," Kade said. "Then come back down for dinner."

"Whatever." Riley grabbed up his backpack and stomped up the stairs.

Meg grimaced. "Thanks."

"He's going through a rough period, but I've found that stating what I want and following through helps." Kade set the suitcase he was carrying at the foot of the stairs. "Here's more of his stuff. And I brought Neil's mail from the past couple of weeks. There were some bills. I paid them."

Meg accepted the envelopes. "I can pay you back." She needed to figure out what her costs were likely to be, especially since she still had her condo in Denver.

"Don't worry about it."

She eyed him suspiciously. "Why are you being so nice?"

Kade hesitated for a moment, then produced a smile that warmed her to her toes. "Something smells really good."

She had to smile in return. "Meatloaf. You can stay if you like."

"I'd like."

"Let me set another place." Meg returned to the kitchen and pulled another plate from the cupboard. Nothing in there matched, but it didn't matter. Her father's supply of kitchenware definitely required some additions if she planned to cook here. Next time she went to Denver, she'd raid her kitchen.

That thought made her pause. Was she ready to fully move here? To a town filled with dogs? Kade hadn't brought Cutter with him tonight, but she'd encountered far too many other dogs on her grocery trip.

Riley clambered down the steps as noisily as he ascended. "What's cooking?"

"Meatloaf, mashed potatoes, and green beans. Take a seat. You, too, Kade."

The guys wasted no time devouring the meal, even going so far as to have seconds or—in Riley's case—thirds. "I guess you like it?" Meg asked with a smile.

"It's very good." Kade's words rang with an endorsement.

Riley grunted a response.

Kade pinned him with a glare. "Use your words. You're not two."

"It's good," Riley mumbled around a mouthful.

Since the teen was talking, Meg jumped in. "What do you have going this week, Riley?"

He shrugged. "Nothing."

"School starts in a little over a week," Kade added.

"Oh." Meg glanced from one to the other. "Do you need to get school supplies?"

"I guess," Riley muttered.

"The Super Mart also carries school supplies and most everything else," Kade said.

"I noticed that."

"They'll have the list for each school there."

Meg nodded. "How about we go there tomorrow, Riley?"

A touch of anticipation ran through Meg. She'd never been allowed to pick out her own school supplies. Aunt Olivia had usually brought them home for her. "It'll be fun."

Riley gave her a glance that said he didn't think so.

"There's also a big school kickoff picnic at Memorial Park this weekend," Kade added. "It's a final send-off to summer break."

"A picnic!" What fun. Meg couldn't remember her last picnic.

Kade grinned. It was a good look for him. "It'll give you a chance to meet folks. You do have to bring food, though. I can take you and Riley."

"I can walk," Riley said.

"*I'll take you.*" Kade emphasized each word.

A scowl filled Riley's face, but Meg nearly clapped with anticipation. "The picnic sounded like an adventure to her, a chance to know Dogwood better, to see the town and meet the residents. "I can't wait."

THE NEXT FEW days with Riley were a challenge, but he was slowly talking to her without his belligerent attitude. Meg enjoyed the school shopping trip, but she couldn't tell if he did. Though he did appear to like his black and gray many-faceted backpack.

She left him home one morning and made a quick trip to her condo to bring back her entire kitchen and some odds and ends. Strange how the condo felt so lifeless after only a few days of living with Riley. And how quickly her father's house was becoming home.

The change to living in a small town hadn't been as boring as she'd expected. In fact, she found plenty to keep her busy, and even enjoyed it. Preparing meals for more than just herself provided a challenge. Kade was right. Riley did like to eat.

She saw Kade almost every night. Apparently, he liked her cooking as well. Since he gave her money toward groceries, she couldn't protest. And she was getting to enjoy his company.

On Saturday, with a picnic basket packed, Meg couldn't deny the thrill inside her. Whether it was due to seeing Kade or the picnic, she couldn't say.

She did have to admit that after the hours she'd spent in Kade's company—mostly talking about Riley—she'd discovered dealing with him wasn't as awful as she'd first thought.

Riley slouched in the rocker/recliner, not so patiently

waiting. "Where is he? Matt and I could have walked there by now."

"He'll be here. It's only ten to ten." Kade had said he'd be there by ten.

As if in response, Meg heard a quick rap on the door and Kade stepped in.

Meg sighed. "I've told you to let me answer the door."

"Never had to before," Kade said. "And I did knock."

"What if I wasn't dressed?" As soon as she said the words, Meg knew it was a bad idea.

Kade's eyes lit up. "I definitely won't knock now."

Heat pooled in Meg's cheeks and she turned away to grab the picnic basket. "We're ready. Let's go."

"'Bout time." Riley pushed up from the chair.

Kade took the picnic basket from Meg, his gaze taking in her clothing. "You're not wearing those shoes, are you?"

She glanced down at her high-heeled sandals. "I don't have much else." She'd needed the right appearance as Ruxton's assistant, and that included the latest designer shoes.

He shook his head. "I was going to suggest we walk, but after lifting this and viewing those shoes, let's drive." He smiled at Meg. "What do you have in here?"

"Lunch."

Riley joined them at the door. "Trust me. We won't be hungry." He rushed outside with Kade and Meg following.

"Says the bottomless pit," Kade said.

When they arrived at the park, Meg couldn't believe how many people—and dogs—filled the lawn. Her pulse hammered as Kade parked the car in the lot. *Deep breath in. Deep breath out.* She'd survived Cutter riding in the back seat with Riley. She could do this.

Riley jumped from the vehicle and ran ahead, Cutter on his heels, until he disappeared in the crowd.

"Riley, wait," Meg called.

"Don't worry. He's off to find Matt." Kade headed in the same direction.

"How will we find him again?"

"He'll come to us when he's hungry."

Probably true. Riley knew this area, these people. Meg didn't.

Though Kade made up for that as he paused to introduce her to several Dogwood residents and their dogs while they searched for an empty picnic table. He knew everyone. He even introduced her to Dogwood's mayor, Dudley Rutherford, a very friendly, almost bombastic man, whose girth almost matched his height. If only there weren't so many dogs. They were all well behaved...so far, but Meg's pulse had kept its rapid beat since she'd stepped out of the car.

"How do you know all these people?" Meg asked in between introductions.

"I've lived in Dogwood all my life." Kade grinned at her. "Stay here long enough, and you'll know them, too."

That idea actually appealed to Meg. Her work with Ruxton had kept her so busy, she hadn't gotten to know very many folks outside of the office. Everyone here was warm and welcoming.

"Kade! Kade! Over here." A woman waved at them from a distant picnic table.

Kade waved back and steered Meg in that direction.

"I'll never remember all these names," she said, trying to keep the panic from her voice. Between the constant presence of dogs and all the new faces, she wasn't sure she'd last much longer.

Fortunately, this woman didn't appear to have a dog with her. Kade set the picnic basket on the table, then enveloped the woman in a warm hug.

Meg fought back an unpleasant sensation. The woman

was fairly pretty, with rounded curves and short curly blond hair. That didn't mean Kade shouldn't hug her. It didn't mean anything.

And why should Meg care anyhow?

But the woman's smile was welcoming and bright, which made her gorgeous. She bestowed the smile on Meg and wrapped her in an unexpected hug. Though surprised, Meg liked it.

"You must be Meg, Riley's sister. I've been dying to meet you." The woman finally released Meg and stepped back, her smile still in place. "I'm Laurel Edison, Matt's mom."

Meg's tension eased at once. Matt's mom. "I've heard a lot about Matt, but not much about you, I'm afraid."

Laurel smiled even wider. "Not a surprise. Matt and Riley have been friends since first grade. Anything not a part of their world doesn't exist." She motioned toward the table. "Come, sit, and join us. The boys will show up when they're hungry."

Kade plopped down. "What did I tell you?"

Meg sat on the opposite side. "I have a lot to learn about teenage boys."

"I'll tell you anything you want to know." Laurel sat beside Meg. "We need to get together more often."

"Oh, no." Kade groaned in mock horror.

"Ignore him," Laurel said with another wave in his direction. "Though I will say he's been a lifesaver for Riley. When Neil died, the bottom dropped out of that boy's life. Thank God Kade was there."

Guilt pressed against Meg's chest. "I didn't even know my father was alive," she murmured. "Or Riley."

"I know you didn't. What a horrible story. I'm sorry you couldn't make the memorial service. Reverend Bannister did a fine job."

"I wanted to be here." In fact, Meg had planned to come,

but Ruxton had made sure that didn't happen. She'd often wondered if Aunt Olivia hadn't played a role in that as well.

"I'm sure you were busy." Laurel poured two glasses of ice tea from a large jug and passed one to Meg. "I understand you have a prestigious job in Denver."

"I had one." But the pain of losing it had lessened considerably in the past week. "I'm looking here now."

"Really?" Laurel's eyes lit up. "What did you do?"

"A little bit of everything." Meg thought back. "The title was Administrative Assistant, but I did everything for Ruxton except create his presentations to the companies. Travel, briefing, scheduling." She paused. "I think mostly I just organized it all."

"Hmm." Laurel tapped the table with her fingernail. "School starts Wednesday. Why don't you come see me at work after Riley goes to school? I might have a job for you."

Meg blinked. Finding a job couldn't be that easy. "Where do you work?"

"I own my business, such as it is."

"She's well known around here for her ability to make things look great on a budget," Kade added.

Meg glanced between the two in puzzlement. "So how does that relate?"

"I'm an interior designer. I love that part of it, but I'm falling behind on the paperwork side of things. Come take a look and tell me if I can be organized, and we'll see where it goes from there."

"That sounds like a plan." A position organizing a business? Exactly her forte. She couldn't believe she might have fallen into the perfect situation. Meg wanted to pinch herself.

"If I'd known you were looking for a job, I would have helped." Kade raised the lid of Meg's picnic basket. "Look at all this stuff. Is it too much to hope that there's a beer in there?"

"Actually, I didn't think about it." She'd never been much of a drinker.

"I have some," Laurel said.

Kade sent the woman his knee-melting smile. "You've saved my life."

Laurel rolled her eyes. "Yeah, right."

She pulled a beer from her cooler to give him, then grabbed another one when Steve appeared a few minutes later.

He brushed a light kiss on her cheek. "You're going to make some man very happy, L."

"So you say." Laurel turned away but Meg caught a glimpse of the blush that tinted her cheeks.

Hmmm, was Laurel interested in Steve? Meg cast a look at Laurel's hand. No ring. Apparently, Matt's father wasn't in the picture.

The boys burst in shortly after that, along with Cutter, and made short work of both picnic baskets with only a little help from the adults. Cutter sat by them, eager for the hand-outs from Riley. Meg made sure she sat at the opposite end of the table.

Meg liked Matt. She'd seen him earlier in the week, but this was her first chance to talk to him.

Tow-headed with close-cropped hair, he had his mother's vibrant personality, and talked much more than Riley. With luck, his upbeat attitude would help pull Riley out of his dark periods.

The boys didn't stay long and took off again to join their friends.

The afternoon flew by as Kade, Steve, and Laurel kept a steady banter going, filled with stories about the town and all the latest activities. Though Meg mostly listened, she found her gaze drawn to Kade.

He was a different man than the one she'd first met. This

Kade was relaxed, joking, and smiling a lot more. He appeared more like someone she could picture as her father's best friend. In fact, he reminded her of what little she remembered of Neil—laughing, enjoying life. Kade actually made her like him. Some.

When he wasn't fighting her for Riley, Kade could be good company.

By the time Meg and Kade decided to leave in the mid-afternoon—with Laurel agreeing to see the boys and Cutter home—Meg was able to say good-bye to folks along the way. The stories she'd heard helped to solidify some of the names in her head, such as Bliss Galore and her fiancé, Luke McPherson—from the town's founding families—who were due to get married on Christmas Eve.

They were so obviously in love that Meg experienced a quick sense of longing for that kind of closeness. Odd, she hadn't really wanted that before, but since she'd arrived in Dogwood, she'd experienced many different emotions. She smiled. Maybe because it was the first time her life had slowed down.

"Good day?" Kade asked.

"Wonderful. Everyone here is so nice." Much more so than most of the people she'd dealt with before.

"An advantage—and disadvantage—to living in a smaller place."

"I—" Meg tripped as her heel caught in a divot in the grass. With a gasp, she threw out her arms to catch herself, only to find herself caught in Kade's arms instead

Her breath caught as her gaze met his, his face only inches away. "Those spiky, pointy shoes are a health hazard," he murmured.

"I don't have any others." Meg's response came out in a whisper.

"You'll never be able to hike in those."

"Hike?" She'd never hiked in her life.

Kade slowly set her back on her feet and exhaled. "We're going shopping."

"What?"

He placed the basket in his trunk, then opened the front door of his Jeep for Meg. "Get in." He slid behind the steering wheel and started up the car, pulling away from the curb like a man on a mission.

"Where are we going? Super Mart?"

The glance he sent her was horrified. "For shoes? Never."

Within a few blocks, he stopped his Jeep in front of a small shop. The rugged sign hanging over the front window filled with shoes stated "On the Path" with an image of sturdy boots.

Kade opened his door. "This is where you get *real* shoes."

"Uh huh." Meg followed him inside. She'd never seen so many styles of boots. And not one pair of designer heels.

"Hey, Kade." The older man at the register nodded. "Those Mountaineers aren't in yet."

"Not for me this time," Kade said. "For her." He pulled Meg forward.

The man came out to shake her hand. "You must be Riley's sister. I'm Bill Schofield." He stared at her feet for a moment. "Yeah, those shoes will never do." He led them to a back wall. "But these...you'll love these."

The light-brown boots he indicated were attractive in a rugged sort of way, ending just above her ankles. "If you say so." They looked confining to her.

"Try a pair on." Kade gently pressed her shoulders down so that she sat on a nearby bench. "I'm willing to bet they feel better than those toe-killers."

"We'll see." She turned to Bill. "Size seven."

"Be right back." He vanished into the back of the store.

"You're sure about this?" Meg eyed the display boots. She'd never worn anything like those before.

"Positive. Next step is a pair of jeans. You need to relax. "

She'd worn her plainest pair of black pants and a simple blue blouse, but she'd noticed at the park that she was over-dressed compared to almost everyone else. "Fine. I'll get some jeans."

His grin bordered on wicked. "Good."

Bill returned with a box containing the boots. "Let's try these."

Meg bent to undo the straps on her sandal, but couldn't force the buckle to cooperate.

"Let me." Kade knelt at her feet and worked at the straps. He slid the sandal off, his hand tracing her instep.

Meg drew in a sharp breath. Who knew a man's touch on her foot would send her pulse soaring?

He slid a thick sock on her foot, then loosened the ties on a boot and slid it on. The inside nestled against her foot, soft, not nearly as coarse as she thought it would be. She wiggled her toes. Wow.

Kade finished lacing the shoe, then repeated his actions with the second boot. He held out his hands. "Try walking in them."

He tugged her up and Meg wavered for a moment. The balance was so different. Laughter danced in his eyes. She fought back a smile, but it escaped anyhow.

"I can do this." She stood on her own, then took tentative steps around the carpet. Weird. The snug fit around her ankle was strange, but the boots didn't pinch or rub. She could get used to this. "Not bad."

"Great. We'll take them." Kade followed Bill to the register and removed his wallet.

"I can pay for them." Meg hurried after them. She didn't want to be obligated to him.

"My treat." Kade shot her a quick smile. "Consider it a better welcome to Dogwood."

Meg paused, then went back to grab her sandals and purse. Definitely a much better welcome than his first one.

After leaving the shop, they headed home, Kade pulling into the driveway that separated them. He opened the trunk and Meg pulled out the picnic basket before he could.

"I can get it. It's much lighter now." She glanced at him. "Thank you for a great afternoon, Kade. And for my welcome to Dogwood."

His eyes darkened as she spoke. He captured her face between his hands. "Welcome to Dogwood, Megan."

He brushed his lips over hers, a gentle pressure that sent a flash of heat clear through to her toes.

Before she could do anything more than gasp, he released her and grinned. Probably at her stunned expression.

"Catch you later." He headed for his house as Meg stared after him.

Wow.

CHAPTER SIX

DARN, this wasn't going according to plan. Kade had thought being nice to Meg would win her over to his side. That she'd agree Kade was the best option for Riley.

But the more time he spent with her, the more time he wanted to spend. The kiss last night was supposed to confuse her. It had done that all right, judging from her expression. Problem was, it had unnerved him, too.

Kade shook his head. He'd sworn never to give a woman any power over him. That included the all-too-appealing Megan Grinnell.

As he opened his living room curtains, the scene outside confirmed his earlier guess. Good thing the picnic was yesterday. Heavy, gray clouds filled the sky now, dumping buckets of rain on the town. Small rivers ran through the streets, making their way to the storm drains and, ultimately, the river.

Lightning streaked across the sky, followed moments later by deep, rumbling thunder. A typical late summer thunderstorm that could last most of the day. Fine with him. A good day to crash on the couch and watch TV.

Cutter joined him at the window, and Kade tousled the dog's head. "We're staying in, boy."

Lights already shone from the house next door. Why not crash and watch TV with Meg and Riley? Kade frowned. Hadn't he just told himself to stay away from her?

He still needed to be involved in Riley's life, didn't he? Not allowing himself to hesitate, Kade snatched a jacket from the closet, called for Cutter to follow him, and bolted for Meg's house. She'd been doing better with Cutter around, though she still wasn't comfortable with the dog. Kade needed to work on that.

He only knocked once before yanking open the door to step inside.

Riley greeted him with excitement. "There's an *Aliens* marathon on today," he said. He was used to watching scary movies with Kade, something Meg didn't enjoy as much.

"Sounds like a plan." Kade sniffed the air, the wonderful smell of bacon wafted through the house. "Smells great in here. What's cooking?"

"Pancakes and bacon," Meg answered him from the kitchen. "You're just in time." She set an extra plate on the table with a dry smile. "Amazing how you know when I'm cooking."

"It's better than mine."

"You don't cook," Riley said.

Kade opened his mouth to protest and the boy continued, "Not much, anyhow."

Kade agreed with that. Meal preparation was a necessary evil, and if he could avoid it, he did. "No matter what I cook, it won't be as good as yours, Meg."

She met his gaze, pink blooming in her cheeks. "Sit down and eat."

Yeah, he'd unnerved her all right. If only his chest wouldn't tighten up as well. "Good thing the picnic was yesterday," he said, taking the seat at the table that he considered his.

"Yeah, I bet the river is great right now," Riley added.

"I just hope folks stay away from it." Kade had rescued folks before from the swift current. He leveled his gaze at Riley. "Including teenage boys."

"Yeah, yeah, I know." Riley sat as well and proceeded to pile six pancakes on his plate.

"Can you eat all those?" Meg sat a plate of bacon down as she took her chair.

Riley rolled his eyes at her in response. Kade had seen him put away that much and more. He smiled at Meg, and her answering smile held a rapport that startled him. He didn't want to be sharing thoughts with her. He wanted her to get frustrated and return to Denver.

Didn't he?

He grabbed food to cover his confusion. Time to rethink his strategy.

"Are you two planning to watch movies today?" Meg asked.

"*Aliens* marathon," Riley announced.

"So you've said. I'll pass." Meg only took two pancakes. "I have plenty to keep me busy. Are all your dirty clothes in the hamper?"

Riley shrugged.

That meant they weren't.

Meg obviously understood Riley's actions better by now. "Make sure you do that before movies," she said.

"Whatever."

Riley's standard response, but he did run upstairs after downing enough food to sink a boat while Kade helped Meg clear the table.

He glanced down at her bare feet. "You're not wearing your boots."

"I'm not going outside," she responded with a quick smile.

"Yeah, it's a good day to stay inside." Thunder punctuated his words.

"And watch *Aliens*."

"Well, yeah." Kade winked, then turned toward the couch. His phone rang before he took three steps. He groaned. A call on this type of day was never a good thing.

"Sullivan here."

The commander of the SAR didn't waste words. "We've got a couple trapped along the Great View Trail. Part of it has washed out, and they can't get back. We're deploying in fifteen."

"I'll be there." Kade ended the call with a sigh. "So much for movies."

"What is it?" Concern filled Meg's face.

"A couple trapped on a trail. I need to go. Can I leave Cutter here? He won't be good for this."

Meg only hesitated a moment. "Sure. He'll stay with Riley."

"Thanks."

"Is it safe?"

They both looked at the relentless storm outside. Kade turned for the door. "I know what I'm doing."

She paused to hold the door open, concern in her expression. "Be careful."

He wanted to kiss her. Instead, Kade grinned. "Always."

As he stood an hour later in the pouring rain, studying the washed-out trail along the mountainside, he regretted not stealing that kiss. This wasn't going to be easy. Just getting up the path that was intact had been a slippery trek for him and his three other team members.

Only about ten feet had slid down the slope in a torrent of mud, but the couple they needed to rescue was on the other side, huddled together. Kade looked back at Allen.

"Your turn." Al would fire the bolt to anchor a line across the missing path, then Kade would make his way to the other side with the high line.

Al's first shot missed, the bolt streaming down the slope in the heavy rain. He reeled it back in and shot again. The anchor sank into the hillside.

As Al anchored the line on their side, Kade pulled against the bolt. Secure. So far. Rain this heavy could erode the soil in minutes.

Tightening his helmet, Kade grabbed the line, shifted his backpack, and searched for footing where there was none. He'd done this before. He could do it again. He slid twice, the rope the only thing keeping him from a nasty fall. But he reached the other side, his heart hammering.

The woman was soaked through, her lightweight parka no match for this type of storm. She hugged Kade with obvious relief. "Thank you, thank you."

He nodded. "I'm Kade. We'll have you out of here in no time." Though he wanted to ask why they were out there in the first place, that would come later. He searched for a more solid place to anchor the bolt. Pounding it into rock, Kade fastened the high line and waved back at Al.

Al and Marty hooked up the stretcher and used the pulleys to send it across. The stretcher bounced against the mountainside in the whipping wind, but reached Kade in minutes.

He settled it on the ground and motioned the woman over. "You're first...?" He phrased it as a question and she responded as he'd hoped.

"I'm Lily. He's Ron." She approached the stretcher, her motions tentative. "How does this work?"

"I'll fasten you into the stretcher so you can't fall out, and we'll use it to get you back over there." Kade offered a reassuring smile. "It only takes a couple of minutes."

Lily glanced back at Ron, who nodded at her, rivulets of water pouring down his face. He didn't wear a jacket at all, and looked cold and miserable. "You go first," he told her.

Once she was secured with webbing, Kade guided the stretcher onto the ropes. Within minutes, she reached the other side. Released from the stretcher, she gave Ron a shaky wave.

"You're next," Kade told Ron as the stretcher made its way back.

Ron only nodded, too despondent for words. His trip to safety took a little longer as the wind picked up and banged the stretcher against the mountainside. He reached the other side and once free, was immediately wrapped in a thermal blanket, joining Lily.

Before Kade could make his way back, a loud rumbling echoed overhead. He glanced up to see a torrent of mud and rock cascading his way. "Crap!"

❧ ❧ ❧ ❧

MEG ENDED up watching the first *Alien* movie with Riley, though she hid her eyes through some of it. Blood and guts weren't her thing, and the alien was terrifying.

But Riley loved it, and that mattered. She'd take any kind of bonding she could get. Cutter stayed on the floor at Riley's feet, on the opposite end of the couch.

Cutter was a good dog. He never jumped at Meg, and now that Riley had accepted her, he wagged his tail at her. If she could learn to accept dogs, this one would be a good start.

But not yet.

Cutter jumped to his feet as an emergency alert went off on the TV. Meg pulled back into a tight ball on the couch in response to the dog's movement. She couldn't help it.

But the announcement on the news grabbed her attention away from her rapid pulse.

"...local SAR team rescued Lily and Ron Marshall from the Great View Trail when part of it washed out in the storm. One member of the team was caught in an ensuing slide and is being treated for non-life-threatening injuries." The television showed the rescued couple and some members of the team, but not Kade.

Where was he? Who was hurt? Meg's heart rose into her throat. Was it Kade? She refused to think it. He was all right. He had to be. He'd done this type of stuff before.

Riley jumped to his feet, voicing her worry. "What if it's Kade?"

No. "He's fine," she said to reassure herself as much as Riley.

"But I didn't see him."

"He might have been doing something else when the news was filming." Now if she could convince herself to believe it. She placed a hand against her roiling stomach.

"Call them. Find out."

Call the SAR office? She started toward her purse to grab her phone. Would Kade think she was interfering in his life? Would he be angry that she cared about him?

Meg froze. When had that happened? How had he made her care about him?

She didn't want to be so afraid for Kade. He was trying to take Riley from her. But she did care. She'd care even if she hadn't spent half the night awake, her lips still tingling from his kiss.

She'd been kissed before. But not one of them compared to Kade's.

"Meg." Riley sounded desperate.

"Okay. Okay." Meg acknowledged the panic of his expression. He'd just lost his father. Losing Kade would be like losing his second father.

She raised her phone, but before she could find the SAR number, Kade stumbled through the front door.

"Kade!" Riley rushed to envelop him in a hug as Meg stared. Cutter bounded over with an enthusiastic woof.

Meg wanted to hug him as well. "Are you okay?"

"More or less." Kade hugged Riley back until the boy stepped back with a grimace.

"Were you the one hurt?" Riley asked. "In the rescue?"

"It was wild for a while there." Kade stepped inside, moving slower than Meg had ever seen him.

"You *are* hurt," she declared. Setting her phone beside her purse, she went to guide Kade to the couch, sidestepping Cutter without a thought.

She fought back the urge to hug Kade as Riley had. Instead, she wrapped her arm around his waist and walked with him. His clothes were different—flannel pants and a sweatshirt. He must have gone home to change first. "Sit down," she said.

Kade settled on the couch and Riley plopped beside him. Cutter plopped his head on Kade's lap. Kade ruffled the dog's thick fur.

"What happened?" Riley asked. "The TV said a mudslide."

"Yeah. We'd just rescued the couple when part of the mountain decided to come down."

Meg inhaled a gasp. Though not a hiker, she knew how dangerous the mountains could be. She had to do something for him. But what? "Would you like some tea? Hot chocolate?"

"Not right now," Kade answered with a slow smile. "Thanks."

"So, what happened?" Riley practically bounced on the cushions.

"I was still hooked up, so the rest of the team yanked me toward them. I bounced around a bit, but the worst of it missed me."

"How badly are you hurt?" Meg still stood, arms wrapped around herself, her insides churning.

"Lots of bruises, but nothing broken. My helmet protected my head, so that helped." His half smile sent an arrow straight into her heart. "Wouldn't have hurt anything if it had gotten hit, right?"

"You could have been killed." Meg could only whisper the words.

"Hazards of the job." Kade shrugged, then winced.

She sprang into action, snatching a blanket from the back of the couch to wrap around him. "Here, rest for a while. I'll make some soup later."

"I..." Kade glanced from Meg to Riley. The boy's pleading look must have sealed it. "For a while." Kade glanced at the television. "Hey, I'm in time for *Alien 3*."

"Yeah, Meg's been watching with me."

"Meg?" Kade raised his eyebrows at her.

"When I wasn't covering my eyes," she admitted with a smile. "Go on and lie down. Riley, take the chair. I'll start on the soup."

Riley moved to the chair without argument. Another sign of how attached he was to Kade. Cutter sprawled on the floor along the front edge of the couch.

Meg moved to the kitchen with a soft smile. She prepared the soup, glancing over Kade and Riley occasionally. As the movie progressed, Kade slid lower and lower on the couch until he filled the entire space.

It looked so right. Even with the dog.

How could she ever claim Riley when he was so attached to their father's friend? They had to stay in Dogwood. That much had become obvious.

She needed to figure this out. Somehow.

If only there weren't so many dogs....

By the time Meg deemed the potato soup and yeast rolls ready—good comfort food on a still-stormy day—Kade had fallen asleep, his chest rising with even breaths.

The movie ended, and Riley shut off the television. "Should we let him sleep?" Meg asked.

"Might as well." Riley grinned. He didn't do that often, and Meg's heart warmed. "But I'll eat."

"Of course you will."

Riley polished off two bowls of soup, along with several warm rolls, then headed up to his room. Cutter paused by Kade, as if assuring himself the man was all right, before he followed the boy up the stairs.

Meg sat at the table, her bowl empty, but she couldn't look away from the sight of Kade sleeping on her couch. His black hair fell over his face, giving him a rakish air. The man had no right to look so good.

He mattered—a lot—to Riley. He mattered—not quite as much—to her. And she didn't want him to. She had enough to worry about with taking care of Riley and finding a new job.

She didn't need this man messing with her emotions. She hadn't had much—okay, any—love life. Her job had been her life.

Meg rose to take her dishes to the sink and cover the soup pot. Strange how she didn't miss the chaotic routine of her previous job.

After cleaning up the kitchen, she moved to stand over Kade. Unable to stop herself, she crouched beside him and brushed back a wayward lock of hair. A bruise was appearing on his cheek. How bad were his other bruises?

Her cheeks warmed as she gazed along the length of his

muscular body. Even with clothes and a blanket, he presented a fine figure of a man.

"Like what you see?"

Meg jerked her gaze back to meet Kade's open eyes. A mischievous grin curved his lips. If possible, her cheeks heated even more.

Ignoring his question, she touched his shoulder. "How do you feel?"

"Sore." Kade sat up, snatching her hand when she would have stood, keeping her face close to his. "Were you worried about me?"

"Yes." Meg admitted. "A little." She couldn't let him know he'd begun to matter to her.

"Good." He captured her chin in his hand and stroked his thumb over her lips. His dark gaze captured hers.

Was he going to kiss her again? Meg's heart thudded in her chest. Part of her wanted him to. Part of her was terrified. For a moment, she couldn't speak. She forced words out. "I have potato soup."

Kade dropped his hand with a laugh. "Actually, I need to go home." He allowed her to stand as he pushed to his feet.

"Are you sure?" Could he take care of himself?

"I need a long, hot shower, some aspirin, and my bed," he said.

"That's probably best," she agreed, though she wanted him to stay so she could care for him. She blinked. Where had that come from?

"Better later," he added. He turned toward the staircase. "Riley, I'm leaving. Come on, Cutter."

The boy and dog tumbled down the steps. "I'll see you tomorrow?" Riley asked.

"I'm sure you will." At the door, Kade paused to glance at Meg. "Thanks for worrying."

"Ah..." What did she say to that? "You're welcome."

He smiled, opened the door, and darted out into the still-pouring rain, Cutter on his heels. Meg watched to make sure he reached his house before she closed the door.

"I'm glad he's okay," Riley said.

"Me, too."

At least they agreed on that.

Meg shook her head while Riley headed back to his room. This was not going at all how she'd planned.

CHAPTER SEVEN

"ARE you sure you don't want me to drop you off?" Meg asked Riley as he stuffed all his school supplies into his new backpack.

"I'm very sure," he insisted. "I walk with Matt."

"Okay. Okay." Meg threw up her hands in mock surrender. "Don't let me interfere with tradition."

"That's right," Riley replied with a grin. He joked with her more now. That had to be a good sign. He hefted his pack to his shoulder and yanked open the front door. "See you later."

"Learn new things," Meg added. Aunt Olivia had always told her that. Riley's response was to roll his eyes and shut the door after him.

Maybe not the best thing to tell a fifteen-year-old boy.

Meg had to soothe her own nerves now. Riley had told her how to walk to Laurel's shop, but Meg preferred to drive. She didn't want to arrive all tousled and sweaty for her first job interview in Dogwood.

She smoothed down her black Victoria Beckham pencil skirt and ensured her light green blouse was tucked in evenly. Riley had told her point-blank to lose the jacket that went with it. Meg listened to him. This was Dogwood, after all.

Grabbing her small clutch, Meg placed a hand against her nervous stomach. *I can do this.* Without Aunt Olivia's assistance.

When she arrived at the small storefront tucked away on the backside of the main street, she stopped the car and studied the exterior. A placard in the window stated it was LAUREL'S INTERIOR DESIGN and listed her hours. The only other item in the window was a light wood rocking chair with a large stuffed teddy bear sitting in it.

Cute. It looked like what little Meg knew of Laurel.

When she reached the front door, she found it ajar and poked her head inside. "Laurel?"

"In the back," Laurel called.

Meg stepped inside and saw at once what Laurel meant about being unorganized. There might be some organization to the chaos, but Meg couldn't see what it was. Small boxes were stacked on an easy chair in what she supposed was the customer greeting salon. It also held a settee and coffee table, equally cluttered with envelopes and large cards containing swatches of fabric.

Large, thick binders lined a wooden shelf against the far wall with more binders stacked beside it. Walking farther, Meg encountered a massive L-shaped desk, piled with envelopes that almost hid the monitor on top.

"Wow," she murmured. Laurel really did need her help.

Laurel burst out from a doorframe separating the main room from a smaller room in the back. She held several 12 x 15 inch cards of fabric samples and stared at Meg unseeingly for a moment before her gaze focused. "Meg. Am I glad to see you!"

She set the cards down and rushed forward to give Meg a hug. "You'd never know I run a successful business, would you?" She laughed and motioned at the room around her. "Can I be helped?"

"I'm sure you can." In fact, Meg itched to start organizing things. "But I don't know enough about what you do to know what needs doing."

"It's not really that complicated." Laurel gestured at the binders in the bookshelf. "Most of those flat boxes on the table contain updated samples for these books. They're organized by company. I'm just horribly out of date.

"The smaller binders contain pictures of furniture. The updates for those are in the envelopes."

Meg nodded. "So far, pretty simple."

"I know. Sad, isn't it?" Laurel shook her head with a smile and joined Meg again. "All the papers on the desk just need to get entered into QuickBooks."

"I know QuickBooks."

"Bless you, my child. When can you start?"

"Is that it?" Meg blinked. "Don't you want to see my resume? Ask me questions?"

"Nope. I like you, so I trust you. The pay won't be what you're probably used to, but I can start you at a reasonable amount. We can fill out the paperwork later." Laurel's gaze gleamed with humor. "And I'll let you know if something isn't right."

"I...ah...okay." Meg stared. She had a job. Amazing. "Where should I start?"

"QuickBooks." Laurel removed some envelopes from the chair in front of the computer keyboard and indicated Meg could sit. "See if you can figure out my system. I'll get you some numbers to compare. Have at it."

Meg slid into the seat and placed her fingers on the keyboard to activate the monitor. "Password?"

"You'll laugh at me."

Meg had to grin.

"MatthiasLaurel with initial caps."

Meg did laugh. "Can I change it?"

"Sure. Just make sure you write it down for me somewhere." Laurel turned to the back room. "I have a meeting this afternoon that I'm trying to pull together. Just holler if you need me."

"Okay." Meg studied the monitor. Where would she find the QuickBooks app?

"Oh," Laurel swung back. "You don't have to dress up for me. Jeans are fine." She indicated her own blue jeans and T-shirt. "It can get messy sometimes."

"All right." Meg did need to make a clothing run soon. All she had was business apparel. Working in jeans sounded just fine to her.

Opening the application, she examined the various folders and entries. Yeah, some organization was needed here, too. Excited with the challenge, Meg set to work.

She was so deeply engrossed in her work that a couple of hours later, when a large cat jumped up onto the desktop, Meg jerked back with a gasp, then relaxed. The cat was tiger-striped and heavy-set with penetrating green eyes. He stared at Meg as if expecting something from her.

When she released the mouse, the cat found her hand at once, rubbing its head against her palm. "Ah, so that's what you want." She obliged with pets and scratches until her hand grew tired.

In response, the cat climbed onto the keyboard and sprawled his full-length along it. Miscellaneous keystrokes littered the monitor.

"Oh, no. I don't think so." Meg lifted the cat and set him on the floor. He immediately jumped back onto the desk.

This could be a battle. He stared and Meg returned the stare. "I'm attempting to work here."

He obviously didn't care.

Just as Meg stood to lift him to the floor again, Laurel emerged from the back room. "I see you've met Izzy. He usually comes to work with me."

"Yeah, he's trying to convince me I should pet him rather than work."

"He's good at that." Laurel came over to run her hand along his back and he arched in response. "He does eventually get the message."

Scratching under Izzy's chin, Laurel continued. "It's past lunch time. Want to go to the Blossom Café with me? I'm starving."

At the mention of food, Meg's stomach gurgled. "Sure." The morning had flown by.

They left the cat behind and emerged outside into bright sunshine. "We can cut through the alley." Laurel led the way. "How bad are the books?"

"What you have in there appears to be correct according to the numbers you gave me. I'm reorganizing it somewhat."

"Thank you." Laurel released an obvious sigh of relief. "I hate that stuff."

"I love it."

"This is going to work out wonderfully."

They reached the café in minutes and made their way inside. Only a few tables remained empty, and Laurel waved at Betty as she worked her way over to one. Several folks already seated watched Meg and Laurel until they chose a booth along the front wall. Meg felt gazes on the back of her neck.

"Is it me?" she asked quietly.

"Oh, definitely." Laurel smiled and stood. "Hey, everyone. This is Meg Grinnell. She's coming to work for me as my office manager."

Heat rose in Meg's cheeks when the restaurant broke out in applause. "It's about time," one man shouted.

Laurel waved a naughty finger at him and sat again. "They'll get over it," she told Meg. "You won't get to be new here for long."

Was that a good thing? Meg had to admit she enjoyed Laurel's easy acceptance. "I'm not used to this."

"I wasn't either when I first arrived, especially since I was a single mother, but you couldn't drag me from here now."

Meg hesitated to ask, but Laurel's openness invited questions. "Matt's father?"

"Long gone. He couldn't disappear fast enough when he learned I was pregnant. My family supported me through Matt's birth, but Mom kept pressuring me to put him up for adoption. I couldn't. I left home and came here instead."

"And now you're a successful businesswoman." New respect rose in Meg for the woman who couldn't be much older than she. "It couldn't have been easy."

"There were days," she admitted, "but once Dogwood took me under their wing, I never had to worry again. There's a reason the town's slogan is 'where the best things in life are rescued.' They sure rescued me."

Meg nodded. Could a town full of dogs rescue her? Did she need rescuing? She needed a way for Riley to accept her as his guardian. Doubtful they could do that.

"Now tell me about you and Kade."

"What?" Meg blinked in surprise. "There's nothing to tell."

"I find that hard to believe. I sensed some chemistry between you two at the picnic."

Chemistry? True, Meg liked him better than she had in the beginning. He truly cared about Riley and was fun to be around. And his kiss had sent heat to her toes. But that was an isolated incident.

"We're learning how to be friends. We both want custody of Riley, so it's difficult."

"Yeah, teenage boys can be difficult all by themselves.

Don't worry." Laurel reached across the table to touch Meg's arm. "It will all work out."

"I wish I had your optimism." Thus far, some days were good. Most days weren't.

Betty appeared to take their order, and the talk dissolved into the progress Meg had made on the books. Thank goodness. She didn't want to talk about Kade. She didn't know what their status was. Friends? Enemies? Somewhere in between?

She still wasn't sure that evening when he knocked and popped into her house for dinner—something that was becoming a regular event. Cutter followed on his heels, going at once to lie by Riley on the couch. Kade's bruises had faded to a yellow-green, and he moved better than he had earlier in the week.

"Did you go back to work today?" she asked from the kitchen.

"I tried. They let me stay for about an hour, then booted me out." Kade reached over the couch to tousle Riley's hair. "How was the first day of school, bud?"

Meg turned to listen. Would Kade get more of an answer than she did?

"Okay." Riley replied.

Nope, same two-syllable response. That made her feel better.

"Come on. It was the first day of school." Kade rounded the couch to plop beside Riley. "Did you get old man Riggins for history?"

"He retired."

"What? That's not fair. Every child should have to suffer under Riggins."

Riley grinned and sat up straighter, his interest caught now. Too bad Meg knew nothing about the Dogwood school system. "I got a new teacher. Young, pretty, named Miss

Denard."

"Still not fair." Kade leaned closer. "Real pretty?"

Why did his question make Meg's stomach lurch?

"V-e-r-r-y pretty. I'm gonna like that class."

"What other classes do you have?"

"Trig. Literature with Mr. Magee."

"I'm sorry."

Riley punched Kade's shoulder. "Physics with Mr. Nedermeyer."

"He's good."

"It's physics, man."

Meg couldn't stop her envy. Would she ever have that easy-going relationship with her brother? She turned back to the stove. "Dinner will be ready in five,'" she announced.

'What is it?" Kade asked.

"Goulash."

"Yum. I do love your cooking."

"Only because you're too lazy to cook for yourself."

"Not entirely true." Kade popped off the couch. "I'll even set the table to show my appreciation."

He grabbed matching plates from the cupboard, then paused behind Meg. His heat enveloped her at once, bringing equal heat to her cheeks. "Thanks, Meg."

She felt a brief touch on the top of her head. Was that a kiss? Or what?

He moved away before she could figure it out, and placed the plates, then silverware on the table.

"Good job," she told him. "I'll have you trained yet."

"Never." He shot her a grin.

As they sat eating, Meg dropped her news. "I got a job with Laurel."

Riley's head jerked up. "Oh, man. She'll tell you everything I do."

"I'm hoping so." Meg smiled at him and he rolled his eyes, his most common response lately.

"That's great," Kade added. "Does this mean you're not going back to Denver?"

The tone of his voice was so neutral, she wasn't sure how to answer. "I don't know." She honestly didn't. She needed to sit down and figure out her budget with this new salary and all her expenses—both in Denver and Dogwood. If she stayed in Dogwood, she'd have to give up her condo—the first place that had ever been truly her own.

"I see." Again, that neutral tone. Was he glad, or did Kade prefer she leave? Probably the latter.

"I think I'll like this job," she continued. "Laurel can use my skills."

"I believe that. She's great at what she does, but sometimes she has trouble keeping everything lined up." Kade grinned. "But that's Laurel."

"Have you known her long?"

"Since she moved here." His smile faded. "She was very young and had it rough, but she came through just fine. She's a part of Dogwood now."

"What does it take to become part of Dogwood?" Was there a checklist Meg needed to follow?

Kade shook his head. "I can't really say. Get to know people, participate."

"You really need to like dogs," Riley added.

Meg sent him a glare. "Oh, joy." She picked up her empty plate as she stood.

"We can work on that," Kade said. He helped clear off the table while Riley dashed upstairs to his room.

"I went through counseling for my fear of dogs, and it still hasn't gone away."

He paused beside the sink and faced her. "What happened?"

Meg paused. She didn't like to recall that event, but it wasn't like she ever forgot it either. "I was eight. I'd gone with Aunt Olivia to one of her friends' homes. They had a Rottweiler. At the time, I just thought it was a big dog, and I liked animals."

When she hesitated, Kade placed a gentle hand on her shoulder. Drawing in a deep breath, she continued. "While Aunt Olivia and her friend were talking, I went to pet it. No one said I couldn't. It jumped on me and knocked me down and attacked, biting me. I screamed and Aunt Olivia's friend pulled it away." She shuddered. "I had to have stitches on my arms and face." And Aunt Olivia had derided her for causing a fuss and embarrassing her in front of her friend.

Her hand went to the scar on her cheek. Kade raised his hand to follow her path and traced the mark with his thumb, his touch sending a shiver through her.

"You can barely see it," he said.

"I feel like it's obvious." Meg met his intense gaze, her heart hammering. "The scars on my arms are at least not as noticeable."

Kade took her hands in his and rotated her arms to see the crisscross of faded scars marking them. His grip tightened on her hands for a brief moment. "Come on." He pulled her toward the main room where Cutter lounged in front of the couch. "We need to work on this."

Meg tried to pull free. "I'd rather not."

His gaze was serious. "If you want to live in Dogwood, you must learn to love dogs."

"Is that a law?" She tried to put a teasing note in her voice to cover the rapid beat of her pulse. She'd been getting used to Cutter, but they kept away from each other, too. It worked.

"Just about." He stopped beside the dog and released her hand. Meg took an immediate step back. "Cutter."

The German shepherd leapt to his feet, tail wagging. Cutter was a friendly dog, nothing like that Rottweiler. Meg knew that in her brain, but something deep inside her refused to accept that.

"Sit." Cutter sat at once, tail swishing against the floor. Kade extended his hand. "Shake."

Cutter lifted his paw and accepted the handshake from Kade. Once Kade released the dog's paw, he rubbed the top of Cutter's head. "Good dog."

If the dog's tail could wag more, it did while his mouth dropped open in what some people might call a grin. Meg only saw the teeth. Big, white, sharp teeth.

"I want you to shake his hand now, Meg." Kade extended a hand toward her.

She shook her head, her heart in her throat.

"I swear he won't harm you."

"I know that. I do. But…"

"Trust me. I'll be right here." He wrapped his hand around hers and pulled gently.

Meg sucked in a deep breath. She did need to overcome this phobia, and Cutter would be the perfect dog to help. Still, he was a dog. A big dog. She took a tentative step forward, her pulse hammering.

When she paused in front of Cutter, he cocked his head to look at her. "Good dog." She squeezed the words out through her tight throat.

"Cutter, shake." Kade said.

The dog raised his paw, waiting.

Meg started to extend her hand, then froze. She couldn't. Those teeth.

"Look at his eyes," Kade ordered. "He will never hurt you."

She focused on the shepherd's brown eyes. They were much gentler, more welcoming than his teeth. He kept his paw raised.

"Okay. Okay." Shutting her eyes, Meg took his paw in hers, shook it once, then dropped it and stepped back.

Kade rubbed Cutter's head and neck. "Good dog." Then he turned to wrap Meg in a hug. "Good girl," he murmured, a hint of laughter in his voice.

"Very funny." She pressed her head against his chest, her eyes still closed. His heartbeat was steady, reassuring. He held her firmly, keeping her close. He was warm, and his touch sent warmth pulsating through her.

"That was great," he murmured. "I'm proud of you."

She'd done it. Willingly touched a dog. Even her counselor hadn't been able to get her to do that. She might not do it again in a hurry, but this was a huge step. She glanced up to meet Kade's dark gaze. "Thank you."

"My pleasure." His tone implied more, and he raised one hand to lightly trace the scar on her cheek.

Her pulse quickened. Not from fear this time. His heartbeat increased, too. She could feel it pounding in his chest. He cupped the side of her face, and she leaned into his hand, unable to help herself.

"Meg." His voice sounded deeper as he focused on her mouth.

He was going to kiss her.

And, God help her, she wanted him to.

His lips found hers, gentle at first, then increased in intensity, his arms tightening even more.

There was desire in his kiss that triggered an equal response within her. She wanted...she wanted more. She wanted the kiss to never end.

As he claimed her mouth, he lifted one hand to cradle the back of her head, not allowing her to escape. As if she wanted to.

She wasn't an experienced kisser, but Meg gave back, responding to his demands with equal heat.

With a groan, Kade raised his head and rested his forehead against hers for a moment. "I have to go."

Without another word, he signaled Cutter to follow him and they vanished through the front door.

Meg struggled to control her uneven breathing.

What the heck was that?

CHAPTER EIGHT

By the next week, Kade was back to work, and Meg felt like she was making progress in her new job. The accounts were up-to-date, and she was actually beginning to understand the filing system for all the huge vendor binders.

Today, she sat cross-legged on the floor beside the shelf of binders, a stack of pre-sorted pages sitting beside her. Izzy decided she belonged to him this morning and he curled up in the cradle of her lap.

Absently petting his head, Meg studied the page in her hand. Highmark. Several unusual styles of furniture covered the page. Interesting. Did people actually buy these designs? They must, or Laurel wouldn't carry them.

She leaned forward to snag the book off the shelf and spread it open before her. Izzy twitched at the movement, but didn't budge. Silly cat. With a smile, Meg searched the tabs until she found the one she needed for this product. Replacing the old page with the new one only took moments.

She eyed the stack beside her and picked up the next new insert for this vendor. With luck, she'd finish filing all these today.

Laurel burst into the shop, a wave of kinetic energy in her wake. "You don't need to sit on the floor. I do have chairs. I have lots of chairs."

"This works for me." Meg smiled at her. "How did the meeting go?"

"Wonderfully." Laurel dropped her briefcase on a nearby chair. "We have a new contract."

"Is this for the doctor's office?"

"Yep, for his waiting room. He wants me to check out a new style of chair, though." Laurel paused. "Can I ask you a huge favor?"

"Of course." Laurel had quickly become a good friend as well as Meg's employer. Meg would gladly help her out.

"You don't know what it is yet." Laurel settled on the edge of the desk. "I need to go to Dallas for two to three days. Could Matt and Izzy stay with you while I'm gone?"

"That's fine." Meg stroked Izzy's head. "Matt's a great kid and Izzy is...well, Izzy."

"Exactly. I figured Matt could walk to school with Riley, and you can still bring Izzy into the office."

"That works." Riley would be thrilled to have his friend over. "When do you leave?"

Laurel winced. "Tomorrow?"

"Okay. It's not a problem. Matt can come home from school with Riley tomorrow with his things and I'll take Izzy home tonight." She'd alert Riley tonight.

"You are a lifesaver. I owe you one." Laurel bounced up from the desk. "I need to finalize the rest of this while I remember it." She disappeared into the back before Meg could respond.

Returning to the binders, Meg smiled. The woman never stayed still for long. At least, not that Meg had seen.

Izzy stretched out with a wide yawn, extending over

Meg's lap. She ruffled his belly. "You have no idea what you're in for."

Once she arrived home that night, she set the cat carrier down at the edge of the living room and opened the door to it. Izzy poked his nose out, his eyes wary. After studying his surroundings, he bolted and found a spot under the kitchen table, where in his mind no one could see him.

Riley paused at the bottom of the stairs. "What was that?"

"Izzy, Laurel's cat. I'm watching him for a couple of days." Meg smiled at Riley. "Matt will stay here as well, starting after school tomorrow."

An honest smile spread across Riley's face, bringing a flash of memory. Her brother resembled her father a lot when he did that. "That'll be awesome," he exclaimed.

"It would help if your room is clean enough that he has a space to sleep."

Riley shrugged. "He won't care." But he turned and dashed back upstairs, yanking his cell phone from his pocket as he went.

She grinned. Kade had convinced her that nagging Riley about his room wasn't a battle worth fighting at this point, not while their relationship was still so tentative. But seeing the clutter drove her nuts. Fortunately, he kept his door closed, and she did her best not to look. Riley had learned, however, that if he wanted clean clothes, he got them into the hamper or did them himself. So far, so good.

Turning, she set down Izzy's food and dishes, then set up a litter box for him in the laundry room near the back of the house. As she headed for the kitchen, she mentally listed the ingredients she needed for dinner. Chicken stir-fry tonight. She grabbed the chicken from the refrigerator and placed it on the cutting board. Would Kade show up to eat?

After that bone-melting kiss, she hadn't seen him for several days. He'd only reappeared last night for dinner and acted as if nothing had happened. What was with him? She was only too aware of his presence now, her insides begging for a repeat of that sensual episode. But he acted as if she was only here to steal Riley away.

To heck with all men anyhow.

❖ ❖ ❖ ❖

KADE PACED outside the door to Neil...Meg's house. He should go back home. It was safer there. This woman affected him in ways he didn't want. He'd learned long ago not to trust women, not to give them control over him or his emotions.

So, why was he here?

Because of Meg's cooking?

Partly. Her meals were much better than anything he'd ever cooked. Somehow, she took simple ingredients and made them delicious.

But mostly because he couldn't stay away. He'd tried and found himself peeking out his windows when he heard her car pull into the driveway. Stupid, stupid, stupid.

She needed his expertise on Riley. At least, he told himself that. For now, it worked.

Cutter grew tired of waiting, and pawed at the front door with a whimper, announcing their presence. Blast. He had to go in now.

Kade straightened, knocked, and entered as usual. "What's for dinner?" It smelled good, but then it usually did.

Meg glanced at him from her kitchen, her glance passing over him dismissively before she turned back to the stove. "Chicken stir-fry."

Well, he'd been snubbed.

That's what he wanted, wasn't it?

He'd only taken a few steps inside when Cutter released a low growl. Meg reacted at once, whirling around with a gasp.

Cutter crouched at the corner of the dining room table, his nose poked beneath it. Kade approached him. "What is it, boy?"

Meg started to reply. "Oh, it's—"

Before she could finish, an orange blur erupted from beneath the table, swiping at the dog with rapid movements. Cutter whined and backed away, shaking his head. Plopping down by the couch, he eyed the hissing cat by the table and placed his paws over his injured nose.

Hearing what sounded like sobs from Meg, Kade took a step toward her. "Are—?" He paused. That was laughter, not tears. Meg wrapped her arms around herself, her body shaking.

Kade hadn't heard this type of unrestrained laughter from her before. He joined in without meaning to. "Are you laughing at my dog?" he asked.

"I'm sorry." Meg struggled for air between her laughs. "I've never seen such a large dog taken down by a small cat."

"Small?" Kade eyed the well-fed cat, now grooming itself by the table leg. "I wouldn't say that."

"It's relative." She ventured toward Cutter, a move that surprised Kade. "Are you okay, Cutter?"

He whimpered and lifted his eyes toward her in what Kade called his begging look. Meg hesitated as if debating on petting the dog. She didn't, but that she even considered it was improvement.

"How about a treat?" She returned to the kitchen and found a Greenie for Cutter, one of his favorites.

Another surprise. Kade eyed her. Did he know her at all? She'd bought treats for his dog.

Cutter accepted the treat without hesitation, though Meg

did place it on the floor in front of him rather than letting him take it from her hand. Small steps. Progress.

Kade glanced at the cat. "Is that Laurel's cat?"

"Yep, I'm cat-sitting for a few days. Matt is coming over tomorrow."

"Do you have enough food for two growing boys?" He was completely serious. Those boys could eat.

Meg smiled, her earlier snub gone. "I plan to stock up on the way home tomorrow." She gave him a sideways glance. "Of course, if I didn't have to feed the neighbors as well..." Her teasing tone took the sting from her words.

Kade grimaced. He did eat dinner here a lot, but he left money often, too. "Okay, fine. I'm bringing in pizza tomorrow night."

"That works."

"I suppose you like the vegetarian one," Kade said. It fit the society girl image that she was slowly losing. In fact, seeing her barefoot in form-fitting jeans and a loose blouse made her all the more appealing.

"Actually, I'm a ham and pineapple girl." Meg turned back to the stove. "About ten more minutes."

"I'll set the table." Kade knew where everything was now, and completed the task in a minute, side-stepping Meg as he navigated the narrow kitchen. Almost like a dance, as if they'd been doing it for years instead of just a few weeks.

He shook his head to lose that thought. He was not getting involved with Megan Grinnell. She would leave Dogwood before long. He'd put money on that.

"Are you okay?" Meg gave him a concerned look that slammed a fist into his gut.

His instinct was to go to her and kiss her until she couldn't breathe. Not a good idea. Well, yes, a good idea, but not one he intended to pursue. He turned away from her. "Just fine," he answered.

He paused at the bottom of the staircase. "Riley, dinner in five." The boy's presence would help.

Settling on the couch, Kade petted Cutter. "You okay, fella?"

His nose pain forgotten, Cutter accepted the petting and leaned against Kade's legs for more. "You'll just have to stay away from that mean ol' cat," he added.

"Izzy's not mean, he's a lover," Meg scooped the cat into her arms. He nuzzled her neck, ignoring Cutter's presence.

Kade drew in a deep breath. He'd nuzzle that neck, too, if she wanted him to. No, change that thought. Focusing on Cutter, he pushed that longing away. A dog always loved you, was always there for you. A better deal in the long run.

Riley thundered down the stairs as Meg set the cat down and returned to the kitchen. "Could you pour the milk, Riley?" she asked.

"Okay." The boy sounded less than enthusiastic, but did as she asked.

Progress in that arena, too. There might come a time when Meg no longer needed Kade's advice. That idea bothered him.

A lot.

CHAPTER NINE

LAUREL WOULD RETURN TONIGHT. Meg ran her hand over Izzy's fur as the cat cuddled in her lap. She hated to return the sweetie to his owner.

After almost three days of cat-sitting, Meg found she enjoyed sharing her life with a pet. She'd never before had the freedom or time to spend on an animal.

Maybe now she could.

Yeah, why not? Meg continued to smooth Izzy's back, receiving a rumbling deep purr in response.

The boys clattered down the stairs as the doorbell rang. Meg startled. It was the first time she'd heard it. Kade always knocked and came in.

"Mom's here," Matt announced, pulling the door open.

Laurel entered and wrapped her son in a warm hug. "I missed you," she said.

Though Matt didn't answer in words, his hug appeared equally enthusiastic. Meg lifted Izzy off her lap and into her arms as she stood.

When Laurel released Matt, she aimed for Riley, who ducked away with a grin. "I'm okay," he said.

She pointed a finger at him. "Your time is coming, boy-o." Smiling, she turned to Meg to give her a quick hug that included the cat. "Any problems?"

"None. Matt actually kept Riley busy." True, the boys together made a lot more noise and ate a ton more food, but Meg found their combined energy invigorating. Riley smiled and laughed more when with his friend, and that had to be a good thing.

With reluctance, she passed Izzy to Laurel. "I really loved having him. He slept with me and sits on my lap any time I'm still."

Laurel accepted the cat and nuzzled him under the chin. "Yep, he's my lover."

"I need one of those." Meg liked the snuggling. The image of snuggling with Kade flashed through her mind, sending a flood of warmth through her. She pushed the image away. Better not to go there.

"Riley." She turned to her brother. "What would you think if we got a kitten?"

"A kitten?" He looked at her as if she'd suggested a buffalo.

"I think it's great idea," Laurel said. "You can go to Sanctuary and find your forever pet easily."

"We can go tomorrow, since it's Saturday," Meg added.

"Tomorrow?" Riley continued to stare at her.

"I'd like you to have some input, too."

"I don't know...."

Matt punched his friend in the arm. "Cats are cool, dude. Especially if you get those laser lights and run them up a wall. Even Izzy goes crazy for that."

Riley shrugged. "Okay, I'll go, but I'd rather have a dog."

"You have Cutter."

"He's not mine."

"He thinks he is."

Once Laurel and Matt left, Meg discovered butterflies fluttering in her stomach. This was a big step for her—a pet of her own. Could she do it?

Of course she could. She'd kept her brother alive, if not necessarily happy. A cat should be a piece of cake compared to that. She glanced at Riley's closed bedroom door as she passed it on her way to bed. His music played through it, but didn't blare—a small victory.

Tomorrow would be another big change in her life. Pressing a hand against her nervous belly, she entered her room, already picturing a new member in her family.

🐾🐾

THEY ARRIVED at Sanctuary about mid-morning on the next day after Meg finally gave up waiting for Riley and woke him up.

Though he accompanied her, he presented his usual sullen façade, answering her with monosyllables, if he answered at all.

Didn't matter. She was excited enough for both of them.

A large wooden sign hung at the entrance to the animal rescue complex, announcing it as Sadie's Sanctuary. Bushes lined the long drive and rimmed the half-full parking lot. Sanctuary itself sprawled over several acres and included several buildings. Amazing.

A young woman, slightly older than Meg, met them at the front desk. She took one look at Riley, then extended her hand to Meg with a beaming smile. "Hi. I'm Amber McPherson. You must be Meg Grinnell. I'm so glad to finally meet you."

Meg laughed as she accepted the greeting. "I don't know that I'll ever get used to everybody knowing me."

"Not you so much as Riley." She grinned at him, eliciting a

return smile from his usually deadpan face. "What can I do for you?"

"She wants a kitten," Riley said, warming up to the pretty girl who was way too old for him.

"That's great. We have several right now. Too many, in fact. Just a little paperwork first." Amber guided them through the initial adoption paperwork that ensured Meg was qualified to adopt, then motioned for them to follow her. She led them to a large room dotted with pillows, climbing towers, water dishes, litter boxes, and a variety of balls and toys. "We've just upgraded our cat room with the extra funds we received from the Fourth of July Bachelor Auction."

The rest of the room was filled with cats—all ages, all sizes, all colors and designs. Many of them came running over as Meg and Riley entered, singing a medley of meows.

Meg stared. She'd never imagined so many cats existed in one place. And this was just at Sanctuary.

"We keep the kittens slightly separated." Amber stopped to pet some of the cats as they waded their way to the corner which was set off by a small fence. They stepped over it into a similarly decorated area that also contained cubes in various sizes. "Careful where you walk."

Lively kittens bounded in the space, some hurrying to hide in the cubes, while others immediately demanded attention.

"The fence doesn't really keep the older cats out, but it does enable them to escape from the kittens' abundance of energy if they need to." Amber waved her arm to encompass the area. "We have lots to choose from."

"They're wonderful." Meg sat on the floor and several kittens enveloped her at once. She tried to pet all of them, but couldn't. One after another demanded her attention.

A black kitten used its tiny claws to climb into Meg's lap, and proceeded to make its way up her shirt. "Oh, no, that hurts." Meg had never realized how sharp kitten claws could be. Izzy rarely used his.

Meg plucked the kitten from her shirt and nuzzled it. Tiny mews answered her.

"I want them all," she declared. How could she possibly decide?

Amber laughed. "I understand." After watching Meg play with the kittens, she asked, "Have you ever thought of fostering cats?"

Meg glanced up from cuddling two bundles of fur at once. "What's that?"

"Folks volunteer to take care of some of our cats or kittens that need extra attention. Sometimes it's a kitten too young to be adopted out yet, or medical conditions that require some care."

Meg liked this idea. "Even if I work full-time?"

"You'd have to be able to give medicine, if necessary, and take the cats to the vet."

That wouldn't be a problem with Laurel for a boss. Meg smiled, thankful once again for her new job. She'd never even consider the idea if she still worked for Ruxton. "Can I think about it? I need to see if I can handle *one* first."

"I found our kitten."

Meg glanced around when Riley spoke. She'd forgotten he was there. He cradled an ash-gray bundle of fur to his chest, his expression besotted. "It climbed right up me and started purring. This is the one."

Meg had fallen for all of them, so agreeing to Riley's choice was easy. "Sure." She climbed to her feet to massage the kitten's head. It emitted the loudest purr she'd ever heard from a creature so small.

"Have you picked a name, too?" Judging from Riley's focus on the kitten, he probably had.

"Smoky."

"Okay." Meg smiled at Amber. "I think this is the one."

"Great. Let's go finish the paperwork."

In a short amount of time, Meg found herself the owner of a tiny gray puffball.

While fastening her seatbelt, she smiled at her brother, who still hadn't released the kitten. "You know I wanted this kitten for me," she teased.

His return smile held a touch of sheepishness. "We can share."

"Yes, we can." For that instant, Meg felt like they were actually family. If the kitten helped to bond her with Riley, she was all for it.

After a brief stop to get food and litter, they arrived home to find Kade standing in their driveway.

"Where have you been?" he demanded as Meg exited her vehicle.

She looked at him in surprise. The man didn't own her. "Since when do I have to tell you my schedule?"

He grimaced. "Sorry. It's such a nice day, I thought we could go into the mountains to see the aspens."

"You could have called or texted."

"I just assumed you'd be here."

She pushed the car door closed. "We got a kitten."

"A kitten?" Kade sounded as aghast as Riley had yesterday.

"Yeah, a kitten." Despite his defensive tone, Riley kept Smoky cradled against his chest and he joined them.

Kade looked from sister to brother. "The Grinnells united for once." He laughed at Riley. "I don't know what Cutter will do when he discovers he's been replaced."

"He's not being replaced." As if to prove it, Riley used one hand to motion the dog over.

Cutter bounded over to allow Riley to pat his head. Noticing the kitten, Cutter sniffed at it. In response, Smoky arched his back, fur on end, and hissed. Cutter backed away with a bark.

"This ought to be interesting." Meg turned to the car trunk. "Let me get Smoky's stuff and get settled." She nodded at Kade. "You're welcome to come in."

"Wouldn't miss it."

Once inside, Meg set up the litter box and food dishes for Smoky, then insisted Riley put the kitten down.

He held Smoky closer. "What if Cutter tries to eat her?"

"Then you can intervene, but I think he learned his lesson with Izzy." Cutter was definitely curious, but Meg didn't think he'd harm the kitten.

Boy, is that a change in my attitude. Meg had to smile at herself.

With obvious reluctance, Riley set Smoky on the living room floor. The kitten looked so tiny, especially when compared to the full-grown German shepherd.

Cutter approached her with caution, probably remembering his experience with Izzy. Smoky arched and hissed again, but she didn't swipe at the dog. After a few moments where neither animal moved, the kitten rushed away to the kitchen and the food bowl.

When she emerged, wiping her face on her paw, Riley rolled one of the toy balls toward her. Startled, Smoky arched and jumped sideways about three times.

Meg laughed. What a crazy kitten. She should have done this sooner.

Kade stood beside her. "I like your laugh. You should use it more."

"I think I will." She smiled, watching Smoky as the kitten discovered the small invading ball and decided to teach it a lesson.

"I've got to show Matt." Riley used his to phone to record

Smoky's actions. After a few moments, his phone dinged. "Matt's coming over."

"Okay." Matt had become a part of her family, too.

Riley abruptly scooped up the kitten and ran upstairs. "I'll be in my room." He waved Cutter back when the dog would have followed.

Cutter stopped by Kade, looking desolate, an expression Meg hadn't expected a dog could achieve.

Meg sighed. "That was supposed to be my kitten."

Kade ruffled the rejected Cutter's fur. "He'll get over it in a few days."

She shook her head with a laugh. Having Riley involved was important. Now he felt an obligation to care for the kitten as well. "He wasn't too thrilled with the idea to start with."

"Guess he's changed his mind."

"True. Smoky chose him. I think it makes a difference." She moved to the kitchen to put away the rest of the kitten food.

Kade followed and leaned against the counter. "So, looking at aspens is out for today?"

He sounded as dejected as Cutter looked. Meg sent him an apologetic smile. "I'm afraid so. Tomorrow, maybe?"

"You have Riley and a new kitten. I doubt it."

"I'm sorry." His little-boy sorrow made Meg want to give him a hug.

As if sensing her mood, Kade turned and captured her between his arms against the cabinet. Her pulse jumped as the heat from his body enveloped hers.

"You can make it up to me." A teasing glint mixed with fire in his gaze.

She forced words through her suddenly dry throat. "How is that?"

"Take a walk with me."

Not what she expected him to say. "Now?"

"Sure."

With his face so close, so intense, she needed air. "Okay."

He didn't respond, but his gaze dropped to her lips. With her heart pounding so fast, she couldn't breathe at all.

Just when she thought he'd kiss her, he pushed away and grabbed her hand. "Come on." He led her to the front door and called upstairs. "Ry, we'll be back in a bit."

"'Kay."

He swung open the door to reveal Matt, his arm raised to knock. He stumbled a little.

"Hey!" He shot them an indignant look.

"Sorry." Kade stepped aside and held the door wide. "Come on in. Riley is upstairs."

Matt dashed past and up the stairs without a word. Kade grinned at Meg and tugged her outside, her hand held tight.

"Where are we going?" she asked, her mind still playing catch-up.

"Just a few blocks. There's a small creek nearby that feeds into the river."

"Sounds good." With fall approaching, the temperature was cooler, with some of the trees painting their leaves yellow. Soon, she'd need a jacket at night.

They walked in silence for a while until the creek came into view, cutting a channel behind a line of homes. It ran much shallower than the river, tumbling over small rocks as it flowed.

"It's lovely," Meg said. "So clear." She could see the bottom and tiny minnows swimming. A person could easily wade across it.

"It's always been my go-to place."

Meg found the quiet trickling of the creek soothing. "I see why."

Kade pulled her face him, his gaze intense. "I don't know what to do with you, Megan Grinnell."

Whatever she'd expected him to say, it wasn't that. "*Do* with me?" she echoed. What did that mean?

"I don't want to be attracted to you."

Well, that was pretty blunt. Her heart twisted. "Well then, don't be." She tried to pull her hand free, but he held on.

"I don't want to have this urge to kiss you every time I see you," he continued.

Before she could respond, he captured her face between his hands.

"But I do," he murmured. An instant later, he seized her lips in a kiss so fierce that her knees threatened to buckle.

This kiss demanded a response that she couldn't refuse if she tried. Releasing her face, he slid his hands to her back to pull her tightly against him.

Heat pulsated through Meg's veins, her heartbeat so rapid she could barely breathe. He might not want to kiss her, but she was glad he did.

He made her yearn, want in ways she hadn't experienced before. Her body meshed with his, molding and melting. He kissed her as if they were the only people alive, as if there was no tomorrow, only this moment...now. He ran his hands along her back, snuggling her even closer.

She gasped, her heart pounding. She wanted...she wanted... "Kade."

Breathing heavily, he rested his forehead against hers. "Tell me to go away," he said, his voice rough.

"Why?" She wasn't so naïve as to not know where this kind of passion could lead. She wanted Kade and everything his kiss promised.

"Because I...we...it won't work."

"How do you know that?" Wasn't he willing to even try?

He raised his head, his gaze dulled, and gently pushed her away from him. "I can't do this. I...can't."

"You're being unfair." She'd finally found someone she actually liked—more than liked, wanted to know better. Someone who made her feel wanted.

"I know." He turned away and shoved his hands in his pockets. "I'm not ready for this."

She glared at his back. "Well, let me know when you are."

She brushed past him and stalked back to her house, not daring to look back to see if he followed. The sizzling heat in her body cooled with every step she took.

Blaring music greeted her from upstairs. Matt must still be here. Just as well. She didn't want to talk to anyone right now.

Reaching the living room, she paused. Smoky must have escaped from Riley and come downstairs. Cutter lay sprawled in his usual spot beside the couch, but Smoky nestled against him, her head resting on his paw as they both slept.

A lump rose in her throat. She sensed, more than heard, Kade come up behind her. "If they can get along, can't we?" she whispered.

"Maybe." He ran his hands along her arms, then immediately let go. "Maybe." He cleared his throat and raised his voice to a normal level. "Come on, Cutter. Time to go."

The dog raised his head and looked from Kade to the kitten. He carefully extracted himself despite Smoky's mew of protest.

Meg scooped up the kitten and they watched Kade and Cutter depart. He closed the door after him, leaving a thick silence behind.

She continued to stare at the door as she massaged Smoky's head. "What am I doing to do?"

There was no answer.

CHAPTER TEN

BY MORNING, she knew. She intended to fight for Kade. He mattered to her, and she didn't want to lose that.

She told Laurel as much when she got to work that Monday. "How do I make him fall for me?"

"Oh, honey." Laurel shook her head. "He's already fallen. That's the problem." She continued. "Kade, and Steve, for that matter, both like the ladies, but neither is willing to risk his heart." Some of Meg's frustration appeared in Laurel's expression.

"Why not?" Meg leaned against a table.

"Kade's sworn never to trust women. His mama left him and his father when Kade was about five. Scarred him pretty good."

"She just left? How awful. Has he never heard from her?"

"Not a peep."

Meg could imagine the devastation easily enough. She'd been about the same age when her mother died. At least she'd known her mother loved her, even if she wasn't coming back. To be kept in limbo had to be much worse. "What about his father?" Kade never talked about either of his parents.

"From what I've been told, his papa was a melancholy type who never really got over losing his wife like that. He raised Kade well enough, I guess, but once Kade graduated from high school, his papa took off to look for her."

Meg gasped. Who could do that to a child? "And he's never come back?"

"Nary a peep from him either."

Poor Kade. That explained a lot. "But I wouldn't do that to him."

"You know that, and I know that, but Kade will have to learn that before he'll give his heart."

"What can I do?"

Laurel gave her a warm hug. "Just keep being yourself, hon."

That didn't seem like enough. She sighed. "What did Kade do when his father left?"

"Stayed with Steve and his family for a while, which was good. Steve needed Kade's support not too long after that." A cloud passed over Laurel's face.

"What happened?" Meg touched her friend's arm.

"Apparently, Steve was pretty serious about a girl all through high school. Everyone expected them to get married right after graduation." Laurel turned away, her eyes glistening.

Meg wasn't sure she wanted to know the rest, but she couldn't stop from asking. "And?"

"Shortly after graduation, she was diagnosed with leukemia. She died a year later."

"Wow." Meg couldn't find words. Poor Kade. Poor Steve. She glanced at Laurel. She'd seen the way the woman looked at Kade's friend. "And now you're in love with him."

"We're friends," Laurel protested.

"Uh huh." Meg didn't believe that for a minute. Even Laurel's voice held a different element when she spoke of Steve.

Laurel looked back to give Meg a watery smile. "That's all he wants. Friendship is better than nothing."

"We are in so much trouble." Meg grimaced. "How busy are we today?"

"No visits scheduled."

"Good." Meg snagged her purse and linked her arm through Laurel's. "Let's go to the Dairy Bar. My treat. This calls for a two-scoop hot fudge sundae."

"With extra whipped cream," Laurel added.

"Exactly."

⁂

By afternoon, Meg knew one thing she had to do. She called a realtor in Denver and left a message. Time to give up the condo. Dogwood was her home now. No matter what happened with Kade.

She arrived home, and Smoky roused from her napping spot in the fading sun. The kitten enthusiastically attacked Meg's feet until Meg scooped her up.

"You home, Riley?" she called up the stairs.

"Yeah."

"Spaghetti okay?"

"Good."

Teasing the kitten with one hand, Meg wandered toward the kitchen. She'd meant to start the sauce in the Crockpot that morning, but forgot. She could still pull it together in an hour. It just wouldn't have that slow-simmered quality to it.

She'd set the ground beef by the stove when Kade's familiar knock sounded, followed by his entrance, with Cutter on his heels. Meg eyed them warily. What now?

"I've been called on a rescue," Kade said. "We don't need Cutter for this one. Can I leave him here?"

"Of course." Cutter behaved, and she rarely needed to interact with him. Plus, Riley was upstairs if she needed him. She set Smoky on the floor.

Seeing Cutter, the kitten hissed once, her fur standing on end. Cutter approached and gave her a friendly lick. The hiss changed to a purr as she wound between his legs. "I think we'll be fine," Meg added.

Kade nodded and turned to go.

"Be careful," she added. After his previous incident, she couldn't help but worry about him when he left on one of these missions.

He shot a grin back at her. "Always."

He was gone as quickly as he'd arrived. Meg sighed. She'd make him see he could count on her. Somehow.

Her phone rang as she removed a frying pan from the drawer. Ah, the realtor. "This is Meg Grinnell."

"Hello. This is Randall Everett from Everett Realty. You left a message about selling your condo in the Tower Building?"

"I did."

Riley ran down the stairs. "Was that Kade? I need—"

Meg raised a hand to indicate she was on the phone. "I'd like to sell the place as soon as possible," she continued.

"Do you know how much you owe on it?"

"Not exactly, but I can find out."

"When will it be ready to sell?"

"Almost immediately. There are a few things that need to be done still." She'd have to move everything out and make sure it was clean. Fortunately, she hadn't put much wear and tear on the condo.

"How about if I come by tomorrow to see it?"

The front door slammed and Meg looked around. Was that Riley? Where was he going?

She jerked back to the phone. "Saturday would work better."

They decided on a time and made plans to finish up details then. Meg disconnected and wandered to the front door. She glanced upstairs. No Riley. Opening the door, she looked around outside. Still no sign of him. Weird.

She closed the door and moved to the foot of the steps. "Riley? You there?"

No answer. But that didn't necessarily mean anything. With a sigh, Meg climbed the stairs to the second floor.

Riley's door stood open. That usually meant he wasn't in his room. And he wasn't.

Frowning, she returned downstairs. He knew she was making dinner, and he'd gotten a lot better at telling her where he was going.

She dialed his cell number; it rang into voice mail. "Where are you?" she asked. Disconnecting from that call, she called Laurel, who answered on the second ring.

"Hey, girl. What can I do for you?"

"Is Riley over there? He just disappeared on me."

"I haven't seen him, but let me check with Matt." Laurel must have lowered her phone, but Meg heard her call her son's name. "Matt? Matt?" After a moment of silence, she continued. "Is Riley here?"

"He says no," she told Meg, then broke off abruptly. "Matthias Andrew Edison, I know that face. What aren't you telling me?"

A cold finger traced Meg's spine as Matt spoke in the background, his words indistinguishable. Laurel's exclamation of "What?" didn't help.

"Laurel? What is it?"

"I'm going to let Matt tell you. Yes, Matt, tell Meg. You care about your friend, don't you?"

Meg's stomach clenched. Where was Riley? Had something happened to him?

"Hi, Meg." Matt's reluctance came through clearly. "Ah, Riley...he...um...he ran away."

"What?" Meg lowered the phone for a moment to look at it in disbelief. "Why?"

"He heard you planning to sell the house. He told me no way was he going back to Denver."

"Of all the stupid..." Meg tightened her grip on the phone. "I'm selling the Denver condo, not the house here."

"Oh."

"So, where did he go?"

"He didn't say exactly."

"Matthias!" Laurel's warning tone sounded in the background.

"He...ah...probably went to his thinking spot."

"Where is that?"

"It's just off the Lower Trail."

"And where is that?" Kade had only taken her on one short hike so far.

"You know the small creek down the hill?"

The one Kade had taken her to. "Yes."

"Cross there and the trail starts on the other side."

"I'll find it." Somehow.

"He'll come back before dark," Matt added in a rush. "He knows better than to stay on the mountain at night."

"He'll come home on his own?" She really didn't want to go drag him back unless she had to.

"He will." Matt sounded confident. "I know he will."

Meg glanced at the time. "It'll be dark in an hour or so. I'll give him that long."

Laurel came back to the phone. "He'll come home, Meg," she said. "Or he'll come here, and I'll let you know."

"Thanks, Laurel." After completing the call, Meg went to stand on the front porch. The sun hadn't yet dipped behind the mountains, but once it did, dark would fall in a hurry.

"Come home, Riley," she whispered. Stupid boy. Why didn't he just ask her about the sale?

Dark arrived way too soon as Meg's insides twisted into a mass of knots. No sign of Riley. Cutter seemed to feel her anxiety, and whimpered at her from his spot on the living-room floor.

"Yeah, I know," she replied. Her hands shaking, she punched in Kade's cell number. As she expected, it went instantly to voice mail. He rarely had connectivity when on his rescue missions. She left him a quick message and disconnected, then stared at the phone.

She released a heavy sigh. If she contacted the rescue office, they'd get word to him, but who knew when he'd get back? She had to do something now.

Not allowing any chance of talking herself out of it, she prepared as Kade had taught her. She filled a backpack with water, a first-aid kit and a jacket for Riley, then pulled on her hiking boots and grabbed her own jacket and a powerful flashlight. But she still didn't really know where she was going.

She glanced at Cutter, who met her gaze and thumped his tail against the floor. If anyone could find Riley, it would be Cutter.

She forced herself to pick up the leash Kade had left over a dining room chair. This was important. Riley's life could depend on it. She had to do this.

Her heart pounding, she approached Cutter, who jumped to his feet, expectant. "You're my friend, right?" she asked, her voice only a little shaky.

He dropped his jaw, his tongue lolling out in what she convinced herself was a smile. She tensed as she bent to snap the leash onto Cutter's collar, half-expecting him to snap at her. But he didn't.

Straightening, she sucked in a deep breath. Cutter licked her hand in a comforting gesture and she jerked back.

"It's okay," she told herself as well as Cutter. "It's okay."

She left a quick message with Laurel, then secured the leash around her hand and started for the door. Cutter kept pace with her. "We're going to find Riley."

His ears perked up, his tail wagging. He wanted to find the boy as much as she did.

"We can do this, Cutter." She opened the door, scanned the dark, and together they stepped out.

CHAPTER ELEVEN

MEG HESITATED at the foot of the mountainside, scanning her flashlight along the shrubbery. She'd crossed the small creek that Matt had mentioned, but where did the trail start? There was a lot of land here.

After a moment of searching, she sighed and eyed Cutter, who stood obediently at her side. "Can you find Riley?"

Cutter's tail wagged and he barked once. *Hope this is a good idea.* Meg took a deep breath and unhooked the leash. "Go find Riley. Go find him."

Cutter took off at once, and she hurried to keep up with him. He located the trailhead only a few feet away, and started up it. "Not so fast," Meg called.

In response, the dog paused and barked again. When she caught up, he ventured up the slope again. The dog evidently knew the trail. Meg used the flashlight to find her footing on the uneven dirt path. It might be packed down, but it still had dips and rocks jutting up.

Cutter appeared to know what to do, though. Whenever Meg lost sight of him, he waited until she caught up. "Good dog," she told him, in a gasping breath. Her one hike with

Kade had been pretty easy and on more even ground near the river. This trail climbed up at a steep rate. Why did people think this was fun?

As she struggled to keep up with Cutter, her chest burned, but she didn't dare slow down. Riley couldn't have gone too far. Could he?

Jamming her toes against a rock in the path, she stumbled and caught herself on a nearby pinon tree. "Hold up, Cutter." She pulled in several deep breaths. "Cutter?"

He appeared, tongue lolling. From the way his tail cut the air, he loved this. Of course, he was used to helping Kade. She reached out to ruffle the fur on his head, realizing her fear had dimmed with every step. Finding Riley took priority.

After another deep breath, she nodded. "Let's go."

Cutter led the way, evading the jutting branches with expertise Meg lacked. Though she wore long sleeves and jeans, she suspected she'd still show bruises and scratches after this. A distant sound cut through the darkness. She froze. An animal? She did *not* want to meet a mountain lion on this quest.

Cutter barked in response and shot off. Okay, not a mountain lion. Meg hurried after him. "Riley?" she called. "Riley?"

The sound came again, almost understandable this time. A voice. Riley!

After a few minutes, Cutter barked several times in the distance. Had he found the teen?

Meg pushed herself to keep moving, though each step required a deep breath and the backs of her calves ached. "Riley? Riley?"

"Here."

Closer now. Spurred by the sound of his voice, Meg climbed with new energy. Her brother was here.

Cutter's frequent barks guided her. Not too far. She could do this.

The trail narrowed, one side dropping away into darkness. Not good. She relied on the flashlight more than before to illuminate the rocky path. Placing each step with care, she avoided a large dip in the dirt that could have easily tossed her to the ground.

She navigated around it to be greeted by Cutter's bark. There. Just off the trail. Swinging her flashlight around, she located her brother on the ground beside a jagged rock, Cutter sitting beside him. "Riley!"

She dropped to one knee beside him and wrapped him in a fierce hug. "Thank God you're okay."

To her surprise, he returned the hug with equal strength. As she pulled away, she noticed tear tracks on his cheeks. "Are you hurt?" Or was he just scared?

"I twisted my ankle." He indicated his left leg. "I don't think it's broken, but I can't walk on it."

"Let me see." She unloaded the backpack, passing Riley his jacket which he immediately put on, then used her flashlight to examine his ankle. Definitely swollen and black and blue. "I need to take off your shoe."

He nodded. She could feel him brace as she untied and eased his shoe off his foot. He inhaled sharply, but didn't say anything.

How to tell if it was broken? She had no clue. She ran her hands over his ankle as gently as she could. Nothing felt obviously broken. Well, common sense said to wrap it tight and get him down the trail to a doctor. "I need to wrap it up," she told her brother.

"Okay."

She rummaged in the backpack and pulled out the first-aid kit. It contained a couple of Ace bandages. Those would work. She also grabbed a bottle of water and handed it to

Riley. He guzzled it down in a couple of swallows while she wrapped up his ankle as tightly as she could.

"Does that feel any better?"

"A little," he said. "I'm not sure I can walk on it, though."

"I'll help you." She replaced items in the backpack, then paused as she noticed Cutter. He sat beside Riley, his doggy grin in place. To her own surprise, she wrapped her arms around him in a hug. "You did great, Cutter."

He licked her face in response and, for once, her heart didn't jump into her throat. Drawing back, she found Riley staring at her.

"You hugged a dog," he whispered, a touch of awe in his voice.

She laughed, proud of herself and tickled at his reaction. "So I did. I couldn't have found you without him."

Riley nodded and gave Cutter an equally enthusiastic hug. The dog wiggled in delight, his tail thumping against the hard ground.

Meg laughed, her tension eased. "Let's get you to your feet."

Using the rock and Meg for balance, Riley pushed to his feet, careful not to put much weight on his injured ankle. "I don't think I can go far."

"You can do it." Meg shrugged into the backpack and situated herself under Riley's shoulder. Thank goodness, he wasn't much taller than her. "*We* can do it."

She nodded at the dog. "Lead the way, Cutter."

He jumped into action, but stayed close to them as Meg and Riley navigated the uneven path down. Meg found it as difficult to go down as up, especially balancing Riley. The descent took even longer. They almost fell twice, but managed to keep their uneven footing.

Only a few night noises surrounded them. Since none of

them disturbed Cutter, Meg figured they were okay. The teen boy sweat from her brother about choked her, though.

Meg finally broke the silence. "You know I'm not selling our house."

"You're not?" Riley glanced at her.

"I'm selling the condo in Denver."

He looked away. "Oh." He whispered the word.

"If you had just asked me before running off..."

"I know." He hesitated. "I'm sorry. I really screwed up."

"Yeah, you did." He needed to know that. "At least Cutter was able to help me find you."

"Yeah." He brightened a little at that. "And you came with him."

"You're my brother." Meg gave his shoulders a little shake. "I love you, you idiot."

He didn't reply to that, but she didn't really expect him to. No one said earning his love would be easy.

After several paces down, he spoke again. "I thought no one would find me until tomorrow. Kade is on a rescue, isn't he?"

"He is." Meg sent him a sideways glance. "And he's going to be pissed, too."

Riley grimaced. "Yeah. Am I grounded?"

"Probably. With your ankle, you're not going far anyhow."

After what felt like hours, they reached the bottom and crossed the stream. Meg led Riley to where the road started and stopped. "Stay here. I'll get the car and come for you. You need to go to the ER."

"I don't—"

She gave him her best death stare. "Not open to discussion. You're going."

The boy was smart enough to keep his mouth shut and nodded.

Meg called Laurel with an update from the car, then loaded Riley in the car and headed for the local hospital. The night appeared slow in the ER, and an attendant rushed to bring a wheelchair as Riley hobbled inside with her help. Good. Her shoulder—heck, all of her—was guaranteed to ache tomorrow.

The check-up took time, but she'd expected that. X-rays showed no broken bones. Only a bad sprain as Riley had said. After a couple of hours, they headed home with his ankle freshly wrapped and a pair of crutches.

She pulled into her driveway at the same time Kade entered his. He jumped from his vehicle while she was still opening her door. "Where's Riley?"

In answer to his question, Riley opened the passenger door and struggled to his feet with the crutches. His expression was sheepish as he faced the man.

Kade enveloped him in a hug, then held him back. "What happened?"

"It's a long story," Meg said. "Let's go inside." Her adrenaline gone, all she wanted to do was drop into a chair and stay there.

Coming over, Kade wrapped her in his arms, nestling her close to his chest. Meg rested her head there, enjoying the rapid beat of his heart. She needed this.

"I'll see you inside." Riley opened the back door to release Cutter, then made his way to the house.

"Are you okay?" Kade asked.

"Better than Riley." She didn't bother to raise her head. His familiar scent of pine surrounded her. "How did your search go?"

"We found the person we were looking for." Kade held her back so he could look into her face. "What happened with Riley?"

"He decided to run away because he thought I was selling the house."

"Selling the house?"

Kade's expression of horror made Meg smile. "Yeah, he reacted kind of like that." She pulled away and turned toward the house. "Let's go inside. I really want some hot tea and a comfortable seat."

She let Riley do the explaining while she prepared her tea. The boy sat on the couch, his leg propped up. Kade sat on the opposite end. Riley admitted his stupidity for running away without all the facts. Points for that. As she approached the rocker/recliner with her steaming cup, Riley pointed at her.

"She used Cutter to find me. She hugged him."

Kade looked so surprised that Meg laughed. "You did?" he asked.

"I had to find Riley. Plus, Cutter's grown on me." She patted her lap and the dog rose from his position at Riley's feet and came over to rest his head on her legs. She ran her hand over his head. "I'm still not sure about all dogs, but Cutter is a special case."

Kade's gaze held a warm light as he focused on Meg. "I'm proud of you." He looked at Riley. "For all of this."

"Taught by the best," she said.

"Of course." He grinned. "Now, tell me about selling your condo."

She shrugged. "I realized Dogwood has become home. Riley's here. My job is here. I'm getting to know people. And the mortgage on the condo is killing me."

"That means you're staying here?"

"Yeah, that's what it means." She'd have to explain her decision to Aunt Olivia, who definitely wouldn't understand, but that could wait. Right now, Meg relished the dark heat of his gaze as Kade focused on her.

His slow smile warmed her insides. "Good."

To her surprise, he rose to his feet and pulled her up from the chair, sending Cutter scurrying. Before she could do more than gasp, he kissed her as if branding her with a sign of possession. His possession.

She responded with equal fierceness. This was what she wanted. Him. Somehow, this man had worked his way into her heart, into her life. She couldn't imagine him not being there.

"Oh, gross." Riley groaned. "I'm going to need therapy for this, you know."

Kade broke off to cast a grin over his shoulder. "You'll survive."

Meg struggled to even her breathing, to regain control. "How about something to eat, Riley? And some cocoa?"

"Yeah."

She eased away from Kade with a smile and returned to the kitchen. Nothing fancy. A couple of grilled cheese sandwiches would work. While she cooked, Riley explained his trek up the mountainside and how he tripped and wrenched his ankle. As he admitted to fear when darkness fell along with the night cold and animal noises, her chest ached.

"You're lucky Meg found you," Kade said.

"I know." Riley grimaced. "And yes, I know I'm grounded. How long?"

Kade turned to Meg. "What do you think?"

He was asking for her input. Her chest ached even more with a different kind of love. Did this mean he trusted her now? "Two weeks?"

"Sounds about right."

"Two weeks?" Riley echoed.

"Could be more," Kade added.

The boy sighed and looked down at his ankle. "Guess I'm not doing much anyhow."

"Can you eat?" Meg brought a plate with his sandwich and chips to him. She didn't usually allow eating in the living room, but this was a special occasion.

"Silly question," Riley muttered as he accepted the plate. "Thanks."

"I—" Kade started to speak and Meg handed him his plate with a smile. He cut off his words. "Thanks."

She returned to the kitchen to prepare her sandwich. Her hunger was returning as her nerves settled. She looked into the living room to see the guys eating. Her family.

Yeah, she could get used to this.

HE WANTED HER. Kade looked up from preparing his lessons a few days later. No use trying to deny it. He wanted her. In his life. Forever.

He was so screwed.

Meg had him wrapped him in tendrils he'd long ago promised to evade. How? He couldn't allow this to happen. Couldn't allow anyone to control his emotions like this.

Kade grimaced. He'd done well with that so far, hadn't he?

Maybe if he kissed her until neither of them could breathe, that would help.

Or maybe not.

But he had to do something.

Soon.

AFTER A CRAZY WEEK AT WORK, Meg welcomed Friday night. Laurel had brought in three new jobs, and drafted Meg to help her organize them. Though Meg didn't have Laurel's eye for style, she had enough sense to put the pieces together in an attractive arrangement for presentation to the customer. They made a good team.

With dinner finished—no Kade tonight—and Riley in his

room working on homework despite the music level, Meg flopped on her bed. Would it be a terrible thing if she just went to bed now? Smoky ran in and climbed onto Meg's stomach.

If only she didn't have those tiny, sharp claws when she kneaded. Meg lifted the kitten's paws up, then scratched around her neck. No good. Meg was still a pin cushion. She rolled to her side, snuggling Smoky against her instead.

This time, Smoky concentrated her kneading on the bed comforter. Better.

Glancing around the room, Meg still saw signs of her father. The forest painting on the wall opposite the bed. The wooden valet on top of the tall dresser containing some loose coins and scraps of paper. His cell phone and wallet had gone to Riley. At least, she assumed so, since she'd never seen them.

She eyed the closet. She'd left the door open this morning when she left in a hurry. Her father's clothes were long gone, and hers had replaced them. Tomorrow, she'd go up to Denver and finish cleaning out the condo. Most of it was here anyhow.

Wait. What was that? A box sat tucked back in the far corner of the high shelf. She hadn't noticed it before. It wasn't hers. Maybe her dad's? She'd gotten only tidbits of him from Riley and Kade, not enough to fill in the memories of a young girl.

Curiosity propelling her, Meg stood up and went to the closet. She had to get inside the small room to get to the box, but she finally managed to pull it off the shelf. Not much larger than a shoebox, the cardboard box was fairly light, and she placed it on the bed. What was in it?

She opened the lid to reveal a stack of dusty notebook paper, scribbled with handwriting. An envelope sat on top.

Addressed to her at Aunt Olivia's. It was marked "Return to Sender" in her aunt's familiar scrawl.

Unsealing the envelope, Meg removed the handwritten piece of paper, her heart filling her throat.

LITTLE MEGGY,

Not so little anymore, I suppose. I promised your Aunt Olivia that when she took you to live with her, I wouldn't try to contact you. It's almost killed me, but I kept my word.

But you're an adult now. I should be able to talk to you, to hug you, to see how much you look like your mother. You were headed that way when I last saw you.

Of course, if Olivia sees this before you, you'll never get it. Must keep the Winthrop line pure. But I'm going to try.

Here's my phone number. Just call, and I'll be there as fast as I can. I need a Meggy hug.

With much love,

Dad

A TEAR PLOPPED on the paper. Dad *had* remembered her. He'd loved her, wanted to contact her.

With sobs catching in her chest, Meg read through the rest of the papers. Letters. To her. From a father who loved her very much and never, not once, forgot her. His letters reiterated that often as he told her about his days raising Riley, how much he missed her, how much he missed her mother.

Some letters were angry. *I should never have promised Olivia. A man has the right to see his daughter.*

Some had photos tucked in with them, mostly of Riley as he grew up—from the cuddly toddler she remembered through elementary school, his red hair going from close-cropped to down to his shoulders over the years.

Others were sad. *Will you remember me at all? Will you want to see me?*

The sobs escaped and Meg buried her face in her hands. She could have had a life with her father, could have lived with him if she'd known. Why did Aunt Olivia think it was so important for Meg to follow in the Winthrop footsteps?

Meg had done her part. She'd graduated with honors from high school, taken a prestigious job at a well-known company, mingled with the people Aunt Olivia considered suitable. She'd rebelled occasionally, but not enough.

If she had known this....

"Are you okay?" Riley poked his head into the room.

Unable to speak through the sobs, Meg shook her head and indicated the box of letters. Riley sat on the opposite side of the box and lifted one. He started to read. "Oh."

He read several before he faced her. "I didn't know he'd done this."

"He didn't forget me." Meg sniffled. "He did love me."

"Of course he did." Riley gave her an exasperated look. "Do you know how many times I had to hear, 'Meg did it this way,' or 'your sister always ate her vegetables'?"

"Why didn't you tell me this before?" Meg swiped away tears. "Why did you act as if you'd never heard of me?"

"You were nonexistent to me. Sort of a Santa type of thing to make me behave." Riley grimaced. "Mostly, I didn't care."

Meg stared at him.

"I didn't know." Riley reached across and hugged her. "I'm sorry. I'm sorry."

"He loved you, too." Meg said, savoring his embrace. "There are lots of stories about you in here."

"I loved him." Riley was silent for long time, then he sniffed and pulled back, looking away.

"What is it?" Was he crying, too?

"I loved him, and I let him die."

"What? No, you didn't."

"I was in the car. Right there beside him. I should have done something. Should have helped him." Tears trickled down Riley's cheeks, and he angrily wiped them away.

"Riley, the impact was on his side of car. He died instantly. There was nothing you could have done. Nothing." She cupped his face in her hands. "Do you hear me? Dad would hate it if he knew you were doing this to yourself."

"But I—"

"You loved him, Riley. He knew that. These letters are only a small reflection of that." Meg sniffed back more threatening tears. "He loved both his children always."

Riley stared down at the comforter, the letter in his hand crumpled, then he threw his arms around Meg again. "I didn't want him to die."

"I never once thought you did."

"But I was yelling at him. Wanting to start driver's ed, and he said to wait. Then...then..."

"Oh, Riley." Meg's heart ached for him. No wonder he felt so guilty. "That was not responsible for the accident. The other driver did that."

"But I yelled at him."

"It's not what he's remembering, trust me. I'm sure Mom and Dad are both watching over us, wanting only good things to happen."

Riley lifted a tear-streaked face. "You think so?"

"I know so." And she did. She'd never felt her parents closer than at that moment. "And now we have each other. You have lots of stories about Dad you can tell me."

"I don't remember any."

"Oh, I bet you do. What about your first time horseback-riding?" She'd gleaned that from Dad's letters.

A smile broke through Riley's gloom. "I'm not sure I want to talk about that."

"Here's the deal—I'll tell you something I remember about Mom, and you have to tell me something about Dad. No matter how silly."

"I—"

"Did you know Mom loved to wear high heels? She even cleaned the house in them."

Riley drew back, stunned. "You're kidding."

A sad smile escaped Meg. "I remember watching her dance with the vacuum cleaner. She told me she was practicing for when Dad took her out."

Her brother nodded. "Dad hated jelly. He'd almost shudder when he made my peanut butter and jelly sandwiches. As soon as I was old enough, he insisted I make them."

"Jelly?"

Within an hour, they were both laughing.

CHAPTER TWELVE

"I COOKED TONIGHT." Kade entered Meg's house without knocking, holding two large pizzas in one hand. Cutter followed at his heels. Knowing that she'd gone up to clean out her condo, he figured she'd be tired. Judging by her welcoming smile, he was right.

"You're a lifesaver." She came to retrieve the pizzas, then paused and placed a quick kiss on his cheek with a smile that made him want to pull her in his arms and kiss her properly.

He blinked. Not a bad welcome at all. "Maybe I'll buy pizza more often."

"I wouldn't complain." Riley spoke from where he lounged on the couch. Cutter's ears perked up as he went to plop on the floor by the boy.

"Did you do any work today?"

"Some."

Meg rolled her eyes. "He did hold the door open."

Riley waved toward his ankle. "Hey, man on crutches here."

"He also carried a couple of bags. Very *light* bags," Meg added.

"At least I helped."

"So you did."

Kade watched the exchange and noted how much more at ease the two appeared with each other. Instead of Riley's coolness or sarcasm, he was teasing his sister. Something had happened between them. Riley had accepted his sister.

Was this good or bad? Kade wanted Riley and Meg to get along, but how did that affect his role in Riley's life? He didn't want to lose the close relationship he had with the boy. "Want some help in getting to the table?" he asked.

"Nah." Riley swung into a sitting position and awkwardly got to his feet. Grabbing only one crutch for balance, he hobbled to the dining room table.

"For pizza, he can move," Meg said with a smile. She placed plates on the table around the centerpiece of pizza boxes.

"You know it." Riley lowered himself into a chair and grabbed two pieces of pizza before either Meg or Kade could sit down. "I'm starving."

Shaking her head, Meg exchanged an amused glance with Kade that stunned him. Were they becoming a couple? No. They shared Riley's upbringing. That was it.

A small voice inside told him he was being stupid, but he pushed it away. The intimacy of the moment sent a chill over his skin. No matter how attracted he was to Meg, he couldn't get serious. No way.

Meg pulled a pizza slice onto her plate. "Laurel invited us all for dinner tomorrow night. Steve is coming, too. Want to go?"

Steve? Though Meg said the statement casually, Kade straightened. Steve might be his best friend, but he'd prefer that Steve and Meg didn't spend much time together. The man was catnip to women.

But no excuse came to mind. "I...ah...I guess so."

"I get to come too?" Riley asked.

"You're part of the family, so I guess we'll have to take you," Meg said.

"Good."

Family? They were a family? Kade's gut twisted. She was getting the wrong idea. Sure, he'd kissed her. He liked kissing her, but family didn't play a part in this at all. He was never getting serious about a woman. Ever.

As soon as the pizza was eaten, Kade helped dispose of the garbage, then turned to the front door. "I...ah...have something I need to do. I'll see ya."

Disappointment crossed Meg's face, and, for a brief moment, he debated on staying. He liked being with her almost as much as kissing her. No, not a good idea. She'd said "family."

"Is dinner still okay?" she asked.

"Sure. Fine." He paused with his hand on the doorknob and motioned for Cutter to join him. "I'll pick you guys up."

Meg nodded. "See you tomorrow then."

"I wanted to show you this cool video game," Riley said.

"Later, dude." Kade escaped outside and drew in a deep breath of the night air. His strategy wasn't working. What strategy? Nothing went according to plan when he was around Meg. And now she had Riley in her corner.

He needed space. He needed her.

Ah, blast.

Forcing himself away from the warm lights of her house, he headed for the darkness of his own.

❖❖❖❖

MEG GLANCED at Kade as they knocked on Laurel's door. The man was a walking contradiction. One moment, he looked at her like she was a hot drink on a cold morning, then the next, he pulled a wall down between them. He was afraid to get involved with anyone. Laurel had told her that. What did it take to convince him Meg wouldn't leave him?

Laurel opened the door and pulled first Meg, then Kade into a warm hug. "I'm so glad you could come." She forced a hug on Riley as he entered, then pointed farther inside. "Matt is waiting for you."

"Yeah." He swung away as fast as the crutches would allow.

"Come on in," Laurel said. "Steve is grabbing a beer. Want one, Kade?"

"That would be great."

"And I have a nice Chardonnay for us girls."

Steve joined them with two beer bottles and extended one to Kade. "I heard you arrive." Once Kade took the bottle, Steve wrapped Meg in a hug. "You've been busy lately."

"That's the truth." Meg smiled at him when he released her. "Who knew living in Dogwood would be so exciting?"

Laurel waved them toward seats. "Just a few more minutes until dinner." She focused on Meg. "When is the condo going on sale?"

"Starting tomorrow. Randall says it'll sell quickly." She'd couldn't quite believe this was happening. A few months ago, she never would have dreamed of leaving Denver. And now she couldn't imagine being anywhere but Dogwood.

"We managed to make a small-town girl out of you after all." Steve raised his beer to her.

"I guess so."

To Meg's surprise, Kade wrapped his arm around her shoulders from his position beside her on the couch. "And she even likes dogs now," he added.

She sent him a wry look and he grinned. "Well, Cutter, at least."

"How is Smoky doing?" Laurel asked, her smile at Meg

full of insider knowledge. Laurel kept telling Meg not to give up on Kade.

"She runs the house," Meg said. "Even Cutter realizes it."

"How about you, Kade?" Steve asked. "Ribs better?"

"A lot better." He extended his arms to display his torso, a sight Meg didn't mind at all. "I'm a fast healer."

"You have to be, to work in rescue," Laurel added.

"It's not usually that dangerous."

"I hope not." Meg placed her hand on his arm. Seeing him hurt once was enough.

A timer sounded and Laurel bounced to her feet. "That's the lasagna. Give me a couple of minutes, and it'll be ready."

"Let me help." Meg jumped up to join her.

"Table is already set, but you can slice up the garlic bread," Laurel said as they entered the kitchen. She paused in setting the lasagna on the stovetop and nodded toward the living room. "Looks like things are going well."

Meg shook her head. "I really have no idea. He's off and on."

Laurel nodded. "Sounds like Kade. He must be terrified."

"Terrified?" That's the last thing Meg would associate with Kade.

"The man is twenty-nine. He's been a bachelor a long time. A woman who can make him give that up has to be really special."

"What makes you think that could be me?"

Laurel smiled. "I can see it. He's falling."

Meg sighed. She wanted to believe that, but when Kade turned chilly, she had a hard time accepting it. "We'll see." She sought to change the subject. "And what about Steve?"

"There's nothing about Steve." Laurel faced the stove again. "I've told you. We're just friends."

"Sure." Meg wouldn't argue, but she wanted to see her

friend happy. Steve just needed a good kick in the pants to see what was right in front of him.

At dinner, she took the opportunity to grill him. Subtly, of course. "Who are you dating now, Steve?"

He looked at her in surprise. "No one at the moment."

"I heard through the grapevine you were seeing Emily Callahan." A pretty young schoolteacher from the Dogwood Middle School.

"We had a few drinks together. Nothing serious." Steve bestowed his award-winning smile on Meg. "She has some growing up to do yet."

Meg knew the woman had finished college before she started teaching. "She has to be a little older than I am."

"Not in years." Steve exchanged a glance with Kade. "You're a lot older than your years, Meg."

"Is that a good thing?" Meg couldn't resist baiting him. Laurel was actually a couple of years older than Steve, not a bad thing in Meg's estimation.

"Depends on the man." Though Steve oozed charm, he produced a patented line.

Kade shot to her defense. "Meg has been through a lot in her life."

Meg shook her head in amusement. What made him do that? "But I've come to Dogwood and found my brother, so my life is great now," she said.

"And you're *staying* here." Kade said the words as if he didn't completely believe them.

"I'm staying here," she confirmed. "In fact, I might see about fostering kittens for Sanctuary. I really enjoy Smoky."

Riley actually showed interest by looking up from his food. "That would be cool."

"I thought we could turn the back room into a kitten den." She'd envisioned the entire thing in her head. It was just a matter of time and money.

"I'll help."

Matt looked at his friend in disbelief. "For cats?"

"Hey, Smoky is okay, and you have a cat, dude." Riley returned to eating, the issue apparently resolved.

Meg laughed. "It won't be right away, so don't worry."

"I'm not sure how Cutter will feel about that," Kade said. "One kitten he can handle. A whole house full..."

"He'll adapt." Would Kade adapt as easily as his dog? Would he want to?

The boys vanished after eating, but the men stayed to clear the table. They then disappeared to the main room while Meg helped Laurel fill the dishwasher and clean up. "I know what you're doing with Steve. Stop it," Laurel said, a warning note in her voice.

Meg nodded with a grimace. Steve would have to figure it out himself. "Men," she muttered.

"Yeah, that." Laurel agreed.

When the women returned to the main room, the men broke off their conversation, their gazes fixing on Meg and Laurel. Laurel placed her hands on her hips. "What?"

"Nothing," Kade said. Meg didn't believe that for a minute.

"Just talking about how great your lasagna was," Steve added.

Laurel eyed him for a moment, then produced a faux curtsey. "Thank you, sir."

"I don't suppose you have any leftovers?" He produced a pitiful look.

"I have a teenage son. No leftovers to give away."

Steve sighed. "I tried."

Meg couldn't resist chiming in. "You'll just have to come eat at Laurel's more often."

"There is that," Steve replied, very noncommittal.

Laurel steered the conversation to games, and, after a few

rousing hands of Uno, Meg and Kade departed, along with a reluctant Riley. Night had fallen, with street lights adding their soft glow to the harsh edges of the darkness.

"It keeps getting dark sooner," Meg said, trying to break the silence in the car.

"It does that." Kade's curt response made her frown. All night, he'd been by her, touching her, and now that they'd left, the wall was back.

Once home, he came in to fetch Cutter, who slept in front of the couch, Smoky curled up against him. Riley hobbled up the steps. "I'll be in my room."

Meg nodded. Good. Once she heard Riley's door shut, she turned on Kade. "What is going on with you?" she demanded.

"Nothing." He headed toward Cutter, but she caught the edge of his shirt and yanked him back.

"Don't give me that. One day you're kissing the daylights of me, the next you're avoiding me completely. I don't know what you're thinking, but I'm not putting up with it anymore. Do you even like me or do you just like kissing the nearest available woman?"

"I—" Kade swallowed. "It's hard to explain."

"Either you do or you don't. And if you don't, you don't have to bother coming over nearly every day."

"It's not that." For once, Kade appeared at a loss for words. "I like you."

"Do you?" Meg whirled away from him toward the kitchen. His words sounded forced, like he didn't want to say them.

"I want to kiss you. A lot."

"What?" Meg looked around, heat flooding her body. Did he really say that?

"You heard me." He took one step, then another toward her, his eyes darkening. "I need to kiss you. I can't help it."

Now she couldn't speak. Her mouth moved, but no

sounds came out. Instead, her body tightened, every nerve on alert.

"What about you, Meg?" He stopped in front of her, his gaze intense. "Do you want that, too?"

She'd never wanted anyone like she longed for him. "I..."

Not giving her a chance to finish, he claimed her lips, his kiss demanding. His hands ran down her arms, then up her back. Her skin tingled, warmed, craved more of his touch.

He cupped her neck and tilted her head to mesh more firmly with his. His lips demanded, then whispered. "Do you want that?" he repeated.

"Yes." She whispered the word. She wanted his hands on her, needed his touch, needed his love.

Kade groaned now and kissed her again, his tongue claiming hers. Lightning zinged along her spine.

"I..." She didn't know what she wanted to say. Don't stop? His kisses made her dizzy, her feet barely felt the floor.

Her world was pounding, reverberating around her.

It took more than a moment to realize the pounding was at the front door. Hard, insistent, unstopping. Along with unending ringing of the doorbell.

Kade glanced at the door. "Ignore it," he murmured, leaning in to seize her lips again.

"I can't." The pounding continued. Sucking in a deep breath, Meg pushed at Kade until he drew back.

She'd get rid of whoever it was quickly.

"I'm coming. I'm coming," she told the outside visitor. Who'd be bothering her now?

"Okay, what do you want?" She yanked the door open. She froze, her heart plummeting to her stomach.

"Oh, my. Aunt Olivia."

CHAPTER THIRTEEN

NOTHING COULD HAVE COOLED Kade's ardor faster than Meg's words. Aunt Olivia! *The* Aunt Olivia?

She stepped through the door, looking exactly as he'd imagined. An old maid who had nothing better to do than control her niece's life. As tall as Meg, the woman appeared in her fifties, her graying hair cut in a fashionable style to frame her long, thin face. The eyes had color, but to Kade, they just looked hard. A classic suit covered her thin figure. She could have come from a board meeting.

"Wha...what are you doing here?" Meg asked, closing the door as if numb.

"I came to talk some sense into you." She eyed Meg's tousled state, then turned her stone-cold gaze onto Kade. "Who are *you*?"

"Kade Sullivan." For the sake of politeness, Kade extended his hand. This was Meg's aunt, after all.

She ignored the offer and he didn't bother to leave it there long.

"I live next door," he said. "I've known Riley all his life."

"Then you could take the boy. There. Problem solved."

Olivia focused on Meg. "Now go pack, you're coming home with me."

"I don't think so," Kade muttered low under his breath.

Meg shook her head as if coming out of a stupor. "No, I'm not."

"What?" Judging from the indignation in the woman's voice, Meg didn't tell her no very often. It was about time she did.

"My life is in Dogwood now." Meg straightened her back. "Riley's here. I have a job here. I have a home here."

"You have a perfectly good condo in Denver."

"I'm selling it." Meg held firm. Kade kept himself from moving to her side. This was her battle, and she was winning it.

"I heard that. Ridiculous. Do you know how difficult it is to find a place like that?"

Meg shrugged. "I'm sure someone else will enjoy it."

Olivia stepped closer so her face was inches from Meg's. "You are coming home now to the life you're meant to live. I'm sure I can persuade Ruxton to give you back your job. That you lost it in the first place shows how you've lost all good sense."

Kade curled his hands into fists by his side. How had Meg put up with this...this creature all these years? He took a step closer to Meg.

She shook her head at him, then met her aunt's deadly gaze. "My home is here. I may be part Winthrop, but I'm also part Grinnell. I'm staying."

"No, you're not." Olivia shouted the words.

Cutter roused from his spot on the floor and came to stand by Kade, his fur on end. A low growl rumbled in Cutter's throat.

Olivia stepped back, her eyes wide. "There's...there's a dog here."

143

"Yes, there is." Meg moved to run her hand over Cutter's head, who responded by licking her hand. "The people here who genuinely care about me have managed in weeks what years of therapy couldn't."

Smoky ambled over, awakened by Cutter's movement. She wound around Meg's legs until Meg picked her up.

"A cat, too?" Olivia acted as if Meg kept tarantulas. "You know I hate pets."

"*You* don't have to live with them," Meg said, petting Smoky until the kitten erupted in her over-loud purr. "*I* like them."

"Oh, it's you." Riley stood at the top of the stairs, the look on his face in complete agreement with Kade's feelings. "We don't want you here."

A snort, almost a smothered laugh, came from Meg who covered her mouth with her hand while Olivia hissed.

"You rude child. Don't you dare talk to me like that."

Riley shrugged. "I'm part Winthrop, too, Aunt Olivia. Live with it."

Ignoring him, Olivia whirled on Meg. "What about all I've done for you? The years I've sacrificed so you could have the best upbringing, the best future?"

The expression on Meg's face softened. "Aunt Olivia, I do appreciate all you've done for me. I really do. But I don't want *your* life. I'm an adult now, and I deserve to live my own life."

Way to go. Kade placed his hand on Meg's shoulder to indicate his support.

Olivia narrowed her gaze, her look of disgust growing. "I see. A man. It's always a man." She sniffed and placed her hand on the door handle. "You'll be sorry, Megan. All men want is one thing from a woman. Don't expect anything more."

She slammed the door after her and a heavy silence filled the house.

"Man, she's intense," Riley said. "Is she gone?"

"I think so," Meg whispered.

"Good." He hopped back to his room.

"You don't need her," Kade said, squeezing Meg's shoulder. He was proud of how she'd stood up for herself.

"I know." She placed her hand over his for a moment, then pulled out of his hold. "I think you should go now. I've lost the mood."

So had he, to be honest. Her Aunt Olivia could kill a party in a heartbeat. "We'll talk tomorrow." Her kisses made him want only more. He called for Cutter, then moved to the door.

"Tomorrow," she agreed.

Her tone left him uneasy. As if she believed what her aunt said.

Kade shifted his shoulders on the walk to his house. Well, yeah, he liked kissing her. But he was more than that. He played a big part in Riley's life, in helping Meg adjust to life here. He just didn't want commitment. He allowed the front door to slam after him as he and Cutter entered.

Yeah, right.

MEG SPENT A RESTLESS NIGHT, torn between the feeling Kade generated within her, and her aunt's cruel parting words. Aunt Olivia meant to hurt her. Meg knew that. But she might be right.

Meg had had to force Kade to say he even liked her. He admitted to wanting to kiss her, but nothing more. She wanted more. She loved him, and Kade didn't give any hint of that. Even when the man infuriated her, she loved him, wanted him in her life.

What if that wasn't what he wanted?

The alarm went off way too early. Groaning, Meg pulled herself out of bed and knocked on Riley's door before she hit the shower.

"Time to get up. School today."

And work. Maybe it would be a slow day.

She'd barely finished getting ready when she heard a knock at the front door. Not Aunt Olivia's impatient hammering, thank goodness. More than likely Kade. He didn't usually come over so early.

When she opened the door, he stood there, his expression indicating he hadn't slept any better than she had. "Kinda early, isn't it?" she asked, turning toward the kitchen. He could come in or not. She needed her tea.

"We left things unfinished," he said, following her.

"Not really." As tired as she was, she wasn't going to mince words.

He looked surprised. "I...ah..."

"No more kisses, Kade."

He examined her face. "Bad night?"

"What do you think?" She put her mug in the microwave.

"You don't believe what your aunt said, do you?"

"I might. What do you want, Kade?" She needed to know. "Kisses aren't enough for me."

"I...ah...what do you mean?" he hedged, and she resisted rolling her eyes.

"You know exactly what I mean. Do we have a future, or is this just a handy-to-have-around kind of thing?"

"What do you mean by future?"

"Oh, quit." Meg sliced her hand through the air. "I care about you, Kade. A lot. But I want more than that."

He stood still. "Meg, I can't."

"Can't what?"

"Give you what you want. I can't commit."

"Why not?"

"You'll leave. I know you'll leave."

"Have I ever given any indication of that?" When the microwave beeped, Meg snatched out her mug, then scalded her tongue on the first sip.

"Women do that."

She stared at him. "You have got to be kidding me. I know about your mother, Kade. What she did was horrible, but I'm not her. I'll never be her. If you really cared about me, trusted me even a little, this wouldn't be an issue."

He hesitated. "You left your job in Denver, left your aunt."

"Oh, no, you don't." Meg pointed a finger at him. "Out. Out now and don't come back. I don't need you. Riley doesn't need you."

"But—"

"Out. Now!" To emphasize her words, Meg stomped to the front door and held it open. "I never want to see you again."

Kade paused at the door. "I can still get custody of Riley."

"Try it." She slammed the door after him, thankful the tears didn't fall until he'd left. Did he really think so little of her? Didn't he trust her at all?

"Was that Kade?" Riley swung down the staircase on his crutches. Looking at Meg, he frowned. "What happened?"

"I don't want him around here anymore." Her words caught in a hitch as more tears threatened.

"You don't mean that." Riley came to face her.

"I have to." No matter what her emotions said.

"But you care about him. I know you do."

"But he doesn't care about me. Not enough."

Riley hesitated, then dropped his crutches to hug her. "I'm sorry, sis."

His use of the endearment refreshed her tears and she clung to him tightly. Finally, she pulled away. "So, what do you want for breakfast? And don't say nothing."

"Toast and peanut butter?"

She nodded. That she could handle.

"I can do it."

"No, I need to do this. Sit down." She poured a glass of juice and placed it on the table before him before sliding the bread in the toaster. Keeping busy helped.

She didn't need a man in her life. She'd manage fine.

"I'll run you up to school in about fifteen minutes."

Riley nodded. The crutches did inhibit his mobility, not matter how well he handled them.

"Maybe we can go a movie or something tonight." She had no idea of what was playing, but that didn't really matter. Keeping active did.

"Sure. There's that new movie with the Dwayne Johnson I'd like to see."

"That's fine." She enjoyed that actor as well. "I'll check times once I get to work."

By the time she'd finished preparing for the day and cleaning up from breakfast, Meg was ready to leave. The day was definitely going to suck.

Riley swung his backpack onto one shoulder, then maneuvered into place after her. "Am I still grounded this week?" His tone was hopeful.

"Yes." Two weeks, they'd said.

"But Matt can show me some tricks on that new game."

Meg paused. She didn't have it in her to be strict with him right now. "How about Matt comes over after school and shows you here?" A compromise.

"Okay. Yeah, we can do that." Riley threw open the front door, then froze. He glanced back at Meg.

148

"What is—? Oh." The last person she ever expected to see again stood on her doorstep. "Ruxton."

He nodded, his manner as regal as ever. "We need to talk, Megan. You must come back to work for me. I won't accept no for an answer." He pushed past Riley into the house, then waved a dismissive hand at the boy. "Go on wherever you were going."

"I was taking him to school." Meg struggled to find the words. Ruxton always intimidated her in person.

"He can manage. Go on now." He dismissed Riley as nothing more than a cockroach, and shut the door after him. "Now, listen to me, young lady. It's time for this fantasy of yours to end."

Meg drew in a deep breath. *Oh, help.*

KADE STORMED into Steve's office early. He wasn't about to let Meg take Riley away from him. Steve was still transferring things from his briefcase to his desk. "Can I help you?" he asked, his tone sarcastic.

"I want to get custody of Riley."

"What?" Steve sent a puzzled stare at his friend. "I thought things were going great as is."

"Not anymore." Kade paced in front of Steve's desk. "Meg doesn't want to see me anymore. She'll keep Riley from me."

"Will she?"

"He likes her now." Didn't that explain it all?

"I see." Steve crossed his arms, watching Kade, who continued to pace. "What brought this about?"

"It's complicated."

"Meaning you panicked." Steve's dry tone only irritated Kade more.

Kade paused. "Well, that, but Meg's Aunt Olivia came by last night."

"Oh, really?" Steve sounded interested now. "How did that go?"

"Meg sent her packing. I was proud of her, but then the old biddy warned Meg away from men, said we only wanted one thing and nothing more. And Meg believed her." His exasperation came through clearly.

"Does Meg have a reason not to believe her?"

"Well, I...she knows I like her."

"I see."

Kade whirled on his friend. "Will you stop being a lawyer here and be on my side?"

"I don't think there is a side." Steve shook his head, a sad smile on his face. "Kade, you're my best friend. I love you like a brother. But you're an idiot."

"What?" Where did come from?

"You're an idiot," Steve repeated, then leaned on his desktop to get closer to Kade. "Buddy, you are so head over heels in love with Meg that it's removed your ability to think clearly."

"I..." Steve sounded so sure, Kade hesitated. "I'm not in love with her." His words didn't even convince himself.

"At dinner last night, if I even smiled at her, you looked like you wanted to bash my teeth in."

Kade grimaced. He did have some jealousy issues. Meg would leave him for Steve in a heartbeat. "Women love you."

"And I love them." Steve grinned. "But I only love Meg as a good friend because my best friend is in love with her and she's in love with you."

"She's in love with me?" True, she'd said she cared about him. "She'll end up leaving."

"No, she won't. Meg is not your mother." Steve pushed back to stand again. "Do you know Meg at all?"

"Of course."

Steve didn't say anything. He waited. One of his typical lawyer tricks.

But his words did make Kade think. He hadn't meant what he told Meg about leaving her job and her aunt. In his opinion, she should have done that a long time ago. He admired the way she'd stood up to her wicked witch aunt. Meg was the kindest, bravest, most loyal woman he knew. She'd do anything for her family.

Family.

She considered him part of her family. She'd never leave family. Never.

"Oh," he said.

"Oh," Steve agreed. He rounded the desk and rapped his knuckles against Kade's skull. "I do hope something's starting to work in there again."

Kade shot him an offended glare.

"How would you feel if you never saw Meg again?" Steve asked.

Alarm rose in Kade's chest. "That won't happen. She's staying in Dogwood. You just said she'd never leave."

"Do a 'what if' for me."

Never see Meg again? Kade's panic increased, squeezing his lungs and blocking his throat. He wouldn't accept that. He wanted her. He needed her. Oh, blast, he loved her. "I'm an idiot," he muttered.

"Now we're agreeing." Steve clapped Kade on the back. "What do you plan to do about it?"

"I'll go talk to her." If she loved him, he could salvage this. Maybe.

"Tact is not your greatest skill," Steve said.

Kade gave him a dry look. "I can tell her I love her."

"That would be a good place to start." Steve laughed and hugged Kade. "So, why are you still here?"

Good point. Kade headed for the front door, only to pull it open to see Riley swinging wildly on his crutches toward the building.

"Kade! Kade!"

"What are you doing here?" Kade asked, going to meet him. "Shouldn't you be in school?"

"Meg's old boss showed up. Ruxton what's-his-face. He told Meg she had to come back to work for him. And she was listening to him, Kade." Panic filled Riley's expression. "*She was listening to him.*"

"Meg's got more sense than that." Kade said the words, but didn't quite believe them. She was mad at him, and from what he'd gathered, Meg's old boss had ruled her life for years. From aunt to boss. Now that she'd grown into herself and was free, they were trying to yank her back. "We won't let that happen."

Riley grabbed Kade's arm. "Go talk to her, Kade. Please."

"My car is over here." Kade led the teen to his car then broke the speed limit in heading back to his house.

A sleek, black Ferrari was parked in front of Meg's house. Her boss was still here? Not good.

Kade jumped out of his car as a man came out of Meg's house. Taller than Kade had expected, though not as tall as Kade, Ruxton had dark hair immaculately cut, with hints of gray by his ears. He stood ramrod straight and wore a suit that probably cost Kade's entire month's salary.

Kade intercepted him before Ruxton could get to his car. "You're not taking Meg to Denver."

Ruxton's gaze swept over Kade and dismissed him. "What say do you have in this matter?"

What claim did he have? "I'm the man who loves her." That counted for a lot.

"She can do better than you." Ruxton tried to step past Kade. "She'll come around. She always has."

"Not this time. She's going to marry me." He hoped.

"Not likely."

Kade clenched his fists. He really wanted to plant one in this guy's face.

"Kade, don't." Meg ran toward him from her front porch. "He's not worth it."

Amazed, Kade dropped his fists. Had she been there the whole time?

Meg couldn't believe her ears. He loved her? He wanted to marry her? Where had this man been?

She paused in front of Kade, ignoring Ruxton who moved to the safety of the driver's door on his car, but remained outside.

She met Kade's gaze and took his hand in hers. "Did you mean it?"

"I..."

Definitely out of his element now. Meg grinned. "Do you plan to ask me to marry you?"

"Well, I...yes, but not like this."

"Ask me anyhow." She smiled, slowly.

Kade's gaze darted around, to Ruxton, to Riley, who stood by Kade's car with an amused smile, and back to Meg. She tilted her head. Maybe he wasn't serious, and only wanted to get one over on Ruxton. "If you didn't mean it..."

Kade tightened his hold on her hand. "I did mean it. I just never...this is...I mean. Oh, blast." He raised his other hand to cup her face. "Megan Grinnell, will you marry me?"

He wasn't getting off that easy. "Why should I?"

Ruxton's snort in the background intruded, but she kept her gaze fastened on Kade's.

His eyes darkened. "Because I love you," he said, his voice quiet. "And life without you would be miserable."

Her heart flipped over at least three times. "Do you believe that I'll never leave you?"

"I know you won't."

He sounded so sincere, she threw her arms around his neck. "Then, I guess I'll marry you."

He kissed her at once, gentle, but still possessive. Always that. "Why?" he whispered against her mouth.

She smiled. "For reasons I don't understand, I love you, too."

"Good." Kade kissed her again, longer this time, passion seeping in.

In the background, Meg heard Ruxton's fancy car start up and roar off, but it didn't matter. Only this moment mattered.

Kade loved her.

"Are we really getting married?" she asked.

"Yeah. Yeah." He looked bemused. "We are. And soon."

"Soon?"

A wicked gleam lit his eyes. "In fact, the sooner the better."

Meg laughed. She liked the sound of that.

Riley leaned his crutches against Kade's car and hobbled over, wrapping an arm around each of their necks. "I'm happy for you both," he said.

Meg raised her eyebrows. She'd never expected to hear that from him.

"Honest." He continued, "But I have the most important question of all."

Meg exchanged a puzzled look with Kade. "What's that?"

"Which house are we going to live in?"

Meg and Kade responded at the same time. "Mine."

They laughed and Meg snuggled closer to Kade. "We'll work it out."

READER LETTER

Dear Reader,

I was thrilled and terrified to write in the Dogwood series. All my previous books were paranormal romances, and writing a sweet normal romance provided a challenge. However, once I started writing, the characters came to life and took over the story.

I hope you enjoyed Meg and Kade's romance, along with the adventures of the cats and dogs and teenage boy. It was fun, and I'm onto the next one.

Be sure to look for our Christmas anthology in November. Check out the Dogwood Series Facebook page at Facebook.com/groups/dogwooddevotee/ for the most up-to-date information.

You can find out more about me at my website http://karenafox.com or reach me via email at karen@karenafox.com.

Karen Fox

Monthly Prize Drawing

The series authors will donate goodies to a monthly
Dogwood Delights box, including such things as signed
books and fun pet-related items. We will draw one name at
random from subscribers to our monthly newsletter, the
Dogwood Digest, so if you want to be considered, sign up at
DogwoodSeries.com/monthly-prize-drawing/

Learn More

Visit our Website at DogwoodSeries.com
Join our Facebook Group at
Facebook.com/groups/dogwooddevotee/

And, in appreciation for the work done by animal rescue
organizations, each author will donate a portion of all sales
to one of them.Thanks for reading!

ABOUT THE AUTHOR

Karen Fox knew at age twelve that she wanted to be a writer. She loved putting down on paper the adventures of those characters who came to life in her head so that she could enjoy them over and over. She was much older before she realized that everybody didn't have stories going on in their head and wondered if this made her a little bit weird.

Though she's lived around the country and in Europe with her Air Force husband and three now grown children, she finds it exciting to imagine new worlds, new species, new adventures, and possibilities for the future. This excitement shows itself in her stories.

Upon discovering the local RWA writing chapter in Colorado Springs, Karen sold her first book in 1996 and has gone on to sell several more over the years.

As one who believes by giving, she receives, Karen spent several years in several positions on the local chapter of Romance Writers of America—Pikes Peak Romance Writers, served two terms on the RWA board, and has also served over 20 years with the Pikes Writers Conference.

To date Karen, has published eight paranormal romance books with Kensington, Leisure Books, and Berkley, plus a novella with BelleBooks and a short story with DAW. Her second book, *Somewhere My Love* (now retitled *My Enemy, My Lover*), was a RITA Finalist in 1998. *Prince of Charming*, a paranormal romance, was a winner for the 2001 Award of Excellence in the Paranormal Category and Finalist for the 2001 National Readers' Choice Award. *Buttercup Baby*, another book in the contemporary fae line, went on to win the Booksellers' Best Award.

DOGWOOD SERIES BOOKS

These are in order of publication, but may be read as stand-alones
in any order.

A Match in Dogwood, a Dogwood Romance Prequel
Anthology with seven authors

Chasing Bliss, a Dogwood Romantic Comedy
by Jodi Anderson

Sit. Stay. Love., a Dogwood Romantic Comedy
by Pam McCutcheon

Love at First Bark, a Dogwood Sweet Romance
by Jude Willhoff

Must Love Dogs, a Dogwood Sweet Romance
by Karen Fox

Coming Soon:

Second Chance Ranch, a Dogwood Sweet Romance
by Sharon Silva

A Dogwood Christmas, a Dogwood anthology

Doggone, a Dogwood Cozy Mystery

by Laura Hayden

Welcome Home, Soldier, a Dogwood Romance
by Angel Smits

ALSO BY KAREN FOX

Contemporary Sweet Romances

A Match in Dogwood Anthology

Must Love Dogs

Paranormal Romances

The Hope Chest Series: *The Prince*

The Hope Chest Series Boxed Set

The Three Graces Trilogy: *A Touch of Charm*

The Three Graces Trilogy Boxed Set

Prince of Charming

Buttercup Baby

Cupid's Melody

Impractical Magic

Witch High Anthology: "Late Bloomer" Short Story

Magick Rising Anthology: "Blood Rising" Novella

Sword of MacLeod

My Enemy, My Lover

Made in the USA
Lexington, KY
17 January 2019